Betty's Book
BR
Barbr

JOHNATHON

JO ANN
BURROUGHS

JOHNATHON

Faith Printing
Taylors, South Carolina 29687

Fourth Printing
April 2003

ISBN 0-939241-50-1

The illustration for the cover of *Johnathon* was done by Linda McCaslin, a former art teacher from North Augusta, South Carolina.

For Denny

My husband, my critic, and my friend...

For Todd

My son who inspired me to write about "Johnathon"...

For my precious daughter, Tara,

and my mother

My role models for "Techr"

PREFACE

AS A TEACHER and elementary school principal for the last thirty-one years, I have come to know and love hundreds of children. Most of these children were happy and well-adjusted as they grew and learned from day to day.

But in the midst of the happy, carefree children, were the ones from broken homes, the abused, the neglected, the dirty, the poor, and the unloved. It was because of these children, that I felt compelled to write the story of *Johnathon*.

The character of "Johnathon" is based on a real child who won my heart and support the last year I was a principal. Some of the episodes in *Johnathon* really happened to this little first grade boy who was abused, neglected, and unloved by his parents. The rest of the book is a composite of real life stories that happened to other children during my school years.

It is my hope and prayer that *Johnathon* will cause some teacher or parent or principal or significant other to reach out and make a difference in some child's life. For by reaching out and showing love and concern, we might just redirect a child's life down the path of happiness and success.

Jo Ann Burroughs

JOHNATHON

ONE

I'M STILL TEACHING. I've taught school for thirty-nine years, four months, fourteen days, and seven hours. I've taught six thousand, eight hundred and fifty-seven math lessons; three thousand, four hundred and seventy-four lessons on my community; four thousand, eight hundred and ninety-six lessons on properties; and twenty thousand, five hundred and seventy-one reading groups. I've been to the fire station thirty-eight times and the airport, ten times. I've only missed two days from school in thirty-nine years, four months, fourteen days, and seven hours. One of those days was when my Great Aunt Maude died, and the other was because of...Johnathon.

Ah, Johnathon...in all my years of teaching, I've taught eighty-two Marys, forty-nine Jimmys, fifty-eight Bills, twelve Keishas, twenty-four Brendas, seventeen Kathys, seven Andrews, twenty-nine Steves, fourteen Julies, thirteen Roberts, forty-two Anns, two Todds, three Taras, oodles of Johnnys, but just one Johnathon. Yes...of all the nine hundred and twenty-seven students that I have taught over the years, Johnathon has to be the one I remember the most. I will never forget the first day that he walked into my first grade classroom…

"Techr, Techr, are you my techr?"

I turned from the teachers I had been talking to as I felt someone tapping me on my leg, and I looked down into the dirtiest, most pathetic, little face that I had ever seen. A small, ragtag boy with clothes a mile too big for him and bright, brown eyes, much too large for his little, round face, stood with pigeon-toed feet, lightly tapping my leg.

"Are you my techr?" the little urchin asked, shyly, easing his grimy, little finger into his mouth. "I'm Johnathon."

I said a silent prayer to the good Lord for this awful child to be on another teacher's list as I looked at the new roll that the principal had handed out in the faculty meeting just a few minutes before.

"What did you say your name is?" I asked the child standing before me. "And for Heaven's sakes, take that dirty finger out of your mouth so I can hear you!"

"I'm Johnathon," the little boy repeated, slowly removing the offending finger and hunching his little shoulders and head, as he peered at me with those big, brown eyes, filled with unshed tears. He reached down and grabbed the tail end of his shirt and began to twist it into a tight knot, stretching the already too large shirt out of shape.

"Do you have a last name?" I asked the poor, little creature, as I prayed faster and faster that the Johnathon glaring at me from my class roll was not one and the same.

"It's Adams, Techr. My Daddy said it's a famous name 'cause a presdent had that same name. I bet ya' know all 'bout that presdent, don'cha', Techr?"

My heart flopped down to the pit of my stomach as the name, Johnathon Adams, jumped out at me from my list of children for the school year. I supposed the principal had it in for me by giving me yet another poor, probably dumb as an ox child to endure for a whole year.

"Yes, I guess I am your teacher. Where is you mother, Johnathon? She did bring you to school on the first day, didn't she?"

"My Mommy had to go to work, Techr."

"What about your daddy? Did he come with you?"

"No, Ma'am, my Daddy's sick. He lays in the bed all the time, and he has to take this medcin, and it makes him feel all better. Ya' see, Techr, my Daddy is always sick, 'bout everyday, so's he takes his medcin a lot, and he pours it from this bottle, ya' see, and pours it into a glass and dranks it, and he says it makes him feel all better. But, ya' know what, Techr? My Mommy don't like for my Daddy to take that medcin 'cause she says it makes him mean, and it do 'cause sometimes when he takes a lots of that medcin, he throws thangs at us. But I hide mos' o' the time, 'cept sometimes when I don't have time to hide. But, anyways, I rode the bus to school all by myself!"

I listened to little Johnathon Adams tell about his parents with a sick feeling of dread in my stomach, for I had dealt with his kind before, many times, and I knew what was in store for me. I turned back to my friends who were standing in the doorway of my classroom and continued our conversation when I felt a familiar tapping at my leg again.

"Techr, Techr, do ya' like my clothes?" Johnathon preened himself like a peacock, stretching out the rather faded, Atlanta Braves tee-shirt and smoothing some old jeans that were about three sizes too big for him. "Miss Ada, the lady next door, give 'em to me, and ain't they nice, Techr? How ya' like my hat? Her boy gave me the hat and the shoes, too. Uh oh!"

Johnathon plopped quickly on the floor as he discovered one of his shoelaces was untied. As he twisted the worn laces together, in no way tying them correctly, he prattled on. "My Mommy said for me to keep my clothes real clean 'cause they ain't goin to be no more where they come from, less Miss Ada's boy goes and outgrows 'em agin." Johnathon brushed off the clothes and smiled at me with what appeared to be a toothless grin, pressing his lips tightly together until some white skin actually appeared around his mouth through the dirt and grime.

I shook my head and rolled my eyes back under my lids as I turned back to my friends. They tried to suppress their laughter, but I knew that they were not laughing at what the boy had said. They were laughing at me because Johnathon was on my roll and not theirs.

"Techr, Techr, my Mommy said to 'member to tell you three thangs today."

"And what are those three 'thangs,' Johnathon," I sighed as I once again had a small finger tapping my leg to get my attention.

"Techr, my Mommy said to tell you, let's see, the first thang is...uh, uh...oh, I 'member now! Techr, I'm a pretty smart boy! Techr, I'm my Mommy's smartest boy! I gots a li'l brother, Techr, and he's name Willie, but he ain't smart like me! No, sir! I am sho' smarter than li'l Willie 'cause he ain't ole enuff to talk yet." Johnathon suddenly ducked his little head and looked up at me with those enormous, brown eyes. " But ya' know, sometimes I don't unnerstand what my Mommy wants me to do, and I don't want her to know I don't unnerstand, so I plays like I do so's she won't thank I'm dumb. Techr, can I tell ya' som'em quiet like?"

Johnathon motioned with his dirty little finger for me to bend down to listen to him. "Sometimes, Techr, when I don't unnerstand som'em, will ya' come over to me and help me to unnerstand it real quiet like so's nobody will thank I'm dumb. I sho' don't want folks thankin' I'm dumb, Techr. I see on the TV sometimes these techrs who sit at they desks and shake they fingers at the children and yell, right loud like, 'You git your work done right now fore I give ya' a whuppin'!' You won't holler at me like that, will ya', Techr? 'Cause that would scare me like when my Daddy dranks all that medcin and hollers and stuff. You'll help me unnerstand so's I can be smart in school, won't ya', Techr?"

Johnathon hunched his little shoulders and tucked his chin under again as I straightened up and looked at him, with my sternest teacher-look on my face.

"Johnathon, I will expect you to listen and study like

everyone else in my class. Now find a seat, young man!" As I turned back to my friends, who were snickering loudly by now, the incessant tapping on my leg continued.

"What is it now, Johnathon?"

"Techr, the second thang that I'm 'posed to tell ya' is...uh...uh...uh...I can't 'member that second thang." Grinning broadly, Johnathon continued. "But the third thang is that I'm a purty good boy! I'm a purty good boy, most o' the time, Techr, 'cept sometimes when I don't 'member to be good. Like last night when my li'l brother,Willie, pinched me on my leg, and it hurt, too, Techr. So I hit Willie. I didn't hit him hard, Techr, just a li'l bit hard so he wouldn't pinch me no more. And ya' know what my Mommy did, Techr? She slapped me on my face, and it hurt wurser than my leg where Willie had pinched me."

"Oh, Johnathon!" I reached over and cupped the little face that peered up at me with bright, shiny eyes. " Let me look at your face."

"It's all right, Techr. It ain't nothin' I ain't used to." Johnathon turned his face away from my hand. "Ya' ain't gonna hit me, too, are ya', Techr? 'Specially if I forgit to be good, ya' gonna slap me, Techr, like my Mommy does when I'm bad? I'll try so hard to be good, Techr! I promise I'll try so hard! If I do forgit, sometimes, ya' won't hit me, Techr, will ya'? I git so tired of being hit, Techr!"

I looked back at the other teachers who were still standing in the doorway of my room. They seemed to be captivated by little Johnathon, and, for once, they were really listening to the childish pratter that teachers face daily.

The leg tapping started right back as soon as I looked away from little Johnathon.

"Techr. Techr."

I looked back around at Johnathon who had suddenly become very shy and unsure of himself. Big tears stood about ready to spill out of those big, brown eyes, and his little dirty hands were clinched tightly up to his face.

"What is it now, Johnathon?"

"Techr, my Mommy cried today. My Mommy walked down to the place where the bus stopped for me, and she cried."

"Why did she cry, Johnathon?"

"I don't know, Techr, she just hugged me and cried and said, 'Johnathon, do ya' know why we're making ya' go to school?' And I said, 'I don't know, Mommy. Why?' And she said, 'Cause we want to make ya' somebody important. I don't want ya' to be like us, Johnathon. I want ya' to have a good fewchr, where ya' can have a good job and be happy. Going to school will build ya' a good fewchr."

"Techr, I told my Mommy I didn't know what fewchr meant, and she said that it was what would make me important so she could be proud of me, and she just cried and cried when she told me that." Johnathon clinched his little fists up and wiped away a few, stray tears as he talked about his mother. I got a little misty, too, as I listened to Johnathon.

After a few moments, Johnathon looked up at me.

Wringing his little hands he continued. "Techr, can ya' make me somebody important today so's I can make my Mommy proud when I go home? Can ya' make me a 'specially good fewchr so's I can have a good job and make my Mommy and me happy? Can ya', Techr? Can ya' do it today?"

I looked away, quickly, so Johnathon wouldn't see his stern, no nonsense teacher, crying. The other teachers started to console me about my brand new, pupil problem, when I once again felt the tapping on my leg. When I looked around, Johnathon was slinking away to go to a desk at the back of the room. I could barely make out what he said.

"You didn't hear nothin' I said, did ya', Techr. I know ya' can't hear me when you talking to those other techrs . But I do love ya', Techr."

As I looked at the little, hunched-up figure in the back of the room, I thought I heard a small voice say, "I'm Johnathon."

TWO

AH, JOHNATHON. How he did tug at the strings of my heart that first day of school. I don't know why I didn't give him more attention that day. I guess I figured that he was just another poor, little urchin who wouldn't amount to much. The very idea that he and that pitiful excuse he had for a mother wanted me to make him into somebody important. I figured I'd be lucky just to be able to endure that child for a year!

Most days, I tried to forget that little Johnathon was in my class. But ignoring him was difficult to do. For one thing, he was always dirty. It wasn't long before the other children started to complain about him and didn't want to sit near him.

Finally, after so many complaints, including a few from other parents, I kept Johnathon after school one day to talk to him about his personal hygiene.

"Johnathon, please remain after class so that I can talk to you."

"Why, Techr, I didn't do nothin' bad today, did I?"

"Just stay in the classroom for a few minutes before your bus is called so that I can talk to you, Johnathon."

"Okay, Techr." Johnathon looked at me with a flash of fear in his eyes and started twisting the tail end of that filthy, Braves tee-shirt while the other children rushed out into the noisy halls. I walked to the door to monitor the dismissal for a few minutes. When I turned around, Johnathon was nowhere to be found.

"Johnathon! Johnathon! Where are you?" I didn't have to search very long, because my nose followed the trail of Johnathon's dirty, little body, straight to the back closet. I opened the door, and there was Johnathon, crouching down with his head between his legs, trembling and weeping softly.

"Johnathon, what in the world are you doing in the closet?"

"Please don't hit me, Techr! I didn't mean to take Todd's crayon. I'll give it back. I just took it 'cause ya' said to mark our homework papers with a red crayon , and I didn't have one. I'll give it back. I promise! Please don't hit me!"

"Johnathon! I am not going to hit you! Now come out of that closet immediately, or I will have to send for the principal!"

Johnathon slowly crept out of the closet, still hunched over and darting furtive glances at me out of the corner of his eye. For all the world, he reminded me of a stray animal when it is cornered and doesn't know where to run.

"Johnathon, this is not about the crayon. We'll talk about that later. First, I...uh... want to talk to you about...uh...your...uh...personal hygiene."

" I swear, Techr, I don't have that. Somebody else must o' took that 'cause I sho' don't have it!"

"No, Johnathon, your personal hygiene is not something that you can take. It's something that everyone has...it's how you look and how...clean you are...and how good you smell... and things like that."

Johnathon's little eyes lit up like a light bulb. "So ya' do like my clothes, don't ya', Techr? I just knew ya' did!" Johnathon smoothed the front of the dirty, old shirt and grinned from ear to ear at me.

"Yes, Johnathon, I do like your clothes, but don't you have any others that you can wear while those get washed?"

"I got some, Techr, but they don't fit me no more, so Mommy puts them on li'l Willie now. But Miss Ada's boy's bound to give me some more 'fore long. But these is still good clothes, don't ya' thank, Techr?"

I just couldn't answer Johnathon for a few moments. One set of hand-me-downs was all the boy had? The enormous pity that consumed me suddenly turned to anger as I thought of the sorry parents who had brought this little boy into the world. This was a classic case of child neglect, and I was determined to report such negligence!

"Just go, Johnathon, and catch your bus before it leaves you. Go now. And, by the way, give me Todd's red crayon and get a box of crayons off my desk. And, Johnathon, next time you need something, ask me. Don't take what doesn't belong to you. And don't swear, either!"

"I'm sorry, Techr." Johnathon hung his greasy, little head as he dug into the pockets of those awful jeans and came up with the offending crayon. He slowly handed me the crayon, never looking up and without a word. He then turned and walked out of the room, with his little head down and his hands deep in the pockets of those hand-me-down, filthy, precious jeans!

Tears filled my eyes as I watched Johnathon leave. It was as if something had grabbed hold to my heart and was squeezing it. I walked over to my desk and sat down with what felt like the weight of the world on my shoulders. I was so tired. I stretched out my arms across the desk in order to rest my throbbing head for a few moments before I started planning for the next day, when my hand knocked something on the floor. I looked down to see what had fallen, and there was the box of crayons I had told Johnathon to take with him. Grabbing the crayons, I rushed to the area by the side of the school where the buses loaded each afternoon.

"Has bus number nine already gone?" I asked the teacher on duty.

"It's pulling out now, I believe."

I ran to the bus, but the driver didn't see me in time and pulled out of the school yard. I searched the windows on the bus for Johnathon and finally saw him in the very back, looking at me with huge, brown, teary eyes. He just stared at me, not blinking, certainly not smiling. And those eyes…they spoke volumes, because I had just become another angry adult who had crossed Johnathon's path. I turned quickly and went back to my room, carrying the box of crayons that Johnathon had forgotten to take. I knew, without a doubt, that Johnathon Adams wouldn't have his homework again the next day. I don't know why that bothered me so much at that moment. Johnathon never had his homework.

I looked on the calendar to see how many days we had been in school since the first day. Only fourteen days! It seemed like fifty! This was definitely going to be a long year! One hundred and sixty-six more days of Johnathon!

THREE

WHEN JOHNATHON walked into the classroom the next day, he pretty much stayed out of my way. He was still dirty and in the same old clothes, but there was something different about him. For one thing, he didn't tap my leg all day and call, "Techr," and for another thing, he seemed to have lost all enthusiasm for school and especially for me. I called on him several times during the morning, but he just shrugged his shoulders and didn't answer. When I called for homework papers, of course Johnathon didn't have his, and his name went up on the board in the usual place, thus securing his loss of recess again.

I must admit that I only went through the motions of teaching that day, and I all but neglected the other twenty-three students in my class. It had finally happened. After five years of being the most straight-forward, get-down-to-business teacher in the school, I had let one dirty, ill-mannered, foul-mouthed, unkempt, little urchin get to me. Ah, Johnathon...how I did hurt for that little tyke.

When recess finally rolled around, I asked one of the other first grade teachers to take my class outside so that I could be alone with Johnathon. When all the children were out the door, I walked back to Johnathon's desk.

"What's wrong, Johnathon? Are you feeling bad today?"

Johnathon didn't answer. He just looked at his oversized, scuffed sneakers as if they had him mesmerized.

"Johnathon, I know why you didn't have your homework today. It was because of the red crayon, wasn't it? You know that I offered you some crayons, though, and you forgot to take them."

"I didn't forgit them, Techr. I just figgerd that since you wuz so mad at me that I better hurry out 'fore ya' hit me." Johnathon peeked at me from under the brim of that old, Braves hat, more hand-me-downs from "Miss Ada's boy," I supposed.

"Johnathon, I would never have hit you! And I wasn't angry at you, Johnathon. I was just angry at…at…oh, I don't know…just angry, that's all." I couldn't tell this poor, little boy that I was angry at his sorry parents. For some reason, he defended them, so I couldn't destroy whatever feelings he had for them.

"Johnathon, look at me." I reached over and touched him on the chin. He quickly turned away. "Johnathon, please look at me." Johnathon eased his tousled head up just a hair and peered at me under his brows. "I just wanted to talk to you about coming to school with clean clothes on and also about taking a bath, too. You do take baths, don't you, Johnathon?"

"Nope, not less Daddy gets to feeling like he needs us all to go to church and get some 'ligion. But he don't thank we need 'ligion much, so's I don't take many baths."

"Johnathon, just how many baths do you take a week?"

"Well, I don't rightly know, Techr. Sometimes after I play with my ole hound dog, George, Mommy makes me and George go take a bath. Did I tell ya' 'bout George, Techr?"

I could see the old Johnathon warming up to me again, so I took a deep breath and answered. "No, I don't believe that you did, Johnathon. Tell me about George."

When the rest of the class came in from recess, Johnathon was still relating the antics of George, the "Wonder Dog," and I was really glad to have recess over for a change. But I had Johnathon back in my good graces, and for that, I was glad.

After school that day, I went shopping. I bought two pairs of size six jeans; two knit shirts, also size six; some little boys' underwear; and a package of boys' socks. A bar of soap, a towel, and a wash cloth were added to the growing list of items in my cart. As I paid the clerk for my purchases, I felt like the proudest parent in the world. One would never have guessed by my actions that day that I did not have any children of my own.

The following day I went to school earlier than usual so that I could have a talk with the school nurse about

Johnathon. I gave her the new clothes and toiletry items, and we secretly planned a bath attack, with a little bribery, for the poor, little fellow. In order for Johnathon to get the new clothes, he had to take the soap, towel, and wash cloth home and take a good bath.

I acted very surprised when Johnathon was called to the office later that morning. After assuring him that he was not in trouble, and that the "Princpal" was not going to hit him, he reluctantly trudged down to see the nurse.

When Johnathon returned a few minutes later, he was empty-handed. He went straight to his desk and sat down, which was unusual in itself, because Johnathon always detoured around the room and delayed sitting if he could help it. Not this time. He sat down and started watching me. If I moved to the left side of the room, his eyes followed me. When I stopped to help another child, those eyes bore into me. Even when I looked directly back at him, the eyes never quit staring.

When recess time arrived, I grabbed Johnathon's hand as I quickly took the other children to the playground and left them under another teacher's care.

"Come on, Johnathon. You have to stay in and do your homework again." Johnathon walked willingly beside me back into the room. But instead of beginning his work, he just stood and continued to stare at me.

"What is it, Johnathon? Why do you keep staring at me?"

"You told her, didn't ya', Techr? You told that nurse lady to make me take a bath, didn't ya'?"

"I...uh...we discussed baths...yes. Are you upset about that, Johnathon?"

"I don't like to take baths, Techr. I just don't like 'em. But I'm going to take a bath tonight, Techr. Can I tell ya' a secret, Techr?" Johnathon motioned for me to lean down so he could whisper in my ear.

"Techr," Johnathon said in a tiny little voice. "Don't tell nobody, but that nurse lady has some new clothes that some people give to the school, and she's going to give some to me if I come to school clean tomorrow. And, Techr, they didn't look like Miss Ada's boy's clothes, 'cause they wuz li'l like me and new-like, so I thank they musta come from some other folks. Can you 'magine folks just giving away new clothes, Techr?"

"Well, Johnathon, I know that people do give clothes to the school from time to time."

"Why ya' reckon they do that, Techr? I know my Mommy wouldn't give nobody no new clothes if we ever had any new ones. I jest don't know why somebody wants to give away new clothes. Reckon' they rich, like the presdent, Techr?"

"Oh, I doubt seriously that the person who gave those clothes to the school is rich, Johnathon. She, or he, just probably wanted to do something nice for somebody else."

Johnathon didn't mention the soap or the towel or the wash cloth that he was to pick up from the nurse at the end of the day. But the next day, he came in smelling like Ivory Soap and grinning from ear to ear. At recess time, when he was supposed to be staying in, again, to do his homework, he went down to the nurse to get his new clothes. When the other boys and girls came back in from playing, a shiny-faced, smiling Johnathon greeted them at the doorway, donned in brand new duds!

Johnathon never knew that I was the one who bought those new clothes for him. He thought some rich person kept him supplied with clothes that entire year. Rich, indeed! On a teacher's salary? No, I was far from rich with money, but somehow I felt like I was rich that year...rich with the unconditional love of a poor, little boy who took over my heart and just wouldn't let it go.

FOUR

EVERYDAY WAS AN ADVENTURE with Johnathon in my class that year. During the first few weeks, he seemed a little slow in the brains department, especially when I compared him to Todd, the principal's kid, who always did everything right, and to Valerie, the minister's daughter who was so bright and well-behaved. I really didn't know Johnathon's parents, for they never came to school to check on him. All I knew was what Johnathon relayed in his childish chatter, and I just didn't know whether to believe all that he told. At any rate, I pretty much labeled Johnathon in the slow average range and placed him in my lowest reading group.

As one day blended into another, and the end of the first six weeks approached, I couldn't help but agonize over the slow progress that Johnathon was making. He never had his homework and always came to school unprepared for the day. When the other children proudly brought in assignments each day, Johnathon usually just put his dirty, little head down on his desk, and watched with those enormous, brown eyes as I called on all the other students to tell about their homework. For a while, I called on Johnathon, too. But as the days passed, and it became increasingly certain that Johnathon would never have his homework, I finally quit calling on him. I tried to tell myself that Johnathon was just another of those students who come along without a care in the world, especially when it involved learning.

Yet, something didn't ring true when I was actually teaching new skills and concepts. At those times, Johnathon's eyes watched me with a bright gleam, and he all but seemed enthralled with grasping what I was teaching each day. When I would question the students about what we were learning, Johnathon constantly yelled out answers, without following the rules to raise his hand. He stayed out of his desk more than he stayed in it, and more often than not, I found myself trying to ignore that Johnathon was there.

Of course, Johnathon stayed in trouble most of the time because of his lack of control. I expected him to behave like the other children, and when he didn't, he had to suffer the consequences. He always had to stay in at recess, not only for neglecting to do his homework, but because of his behavior. He just couldn't control himself; he talked incessantly; and he lashed out at the other students a lot.

Johnathon was picked on and teased by the rest of the class when they thought I was not looking. I often compared him to a pink chicken, all colored up as an Easter chick. Johnathon wasn't pink, but he was certainly different from the others. His appearance and demeanor made him a steady target for the taunts and cruelty that children can inflict upon each other. I tried, half-heartedly, to stop the constant teasing and ridicule that Johnathon endured each day, but because Johnathon was such an aggravation to me, I probably allowed more to go on than I should have tolerated.

Johnathon was like a chronic case of indigestion that just won't go away. I lectured him; I disciplined him; I sent him to the principal; and I ignored him. Well, I tried to ignore him. But that was hardest of all. For all day, everyday, I heard and watched the things that Johnathon did.

"Miz Harris! Johnathon took my crayon!"

"Miz Harris! Make Johnathon leave me alone!"

"Miz Harris! Johnathon smells! Can I sit somewhere else?"

Over and over, as I dealt with Johnathon and listened to his responses about the many accusations, I felt in my heart that something was not right. Oh, I was plenty mad with him many times, but it was more like a parent is angry with her own child. I felt a love for little Johnathon even on his worst days, and believe me, he had many days that were really bad. I'm not sure how many times I let his excuses for his behavior dampen my anger for the little fellow. I believe that I can pretty much recite those excuses from memory.

"But, Techr, I jest needed a yeller crayon. I wuz goin' to give it back!"

"Techr, I wuz jest looking on Todd's paper to see if I had my b's turned the right way."

"But, Techr, you don't call on me if I stay in my seat. I had to yell and jump up for ya' to see me."

Yes, most of the time, Johnathon Adams won me over with his excuses, but mostly, it was the way he looked at me when he tried to explain his actions. I probably wasn't fair to the other children, but there was just something about little Johnathon that kept nagging at me.

Several weeks into the school term, Johnathon missed three days in a row. Even though the days without him were blissfully pleasant, I missed the little fellow and wondered what was wrong. At the end of the third day, I looked in Johnathon's record to see if I could get in touch with his parents. It suddenly dawned on me that we had absolutely no information on Johnathon, except a copy of his birth certificate and immunization card that he had brought in the first day himself. The information sheet that should have been filled out by his parents was woefully blank. I did find an address written on the back of a torn envelope, apparently in the mother's handwriting. Johnathon, probably, had brought that, too, on the first day in order to get enrolled. I copied the address on a notepad and left school a little early that day, with the intention of checking on Johnathon on the way home.

After searching the city map for street names, I headed for the section of town where the address on the torn envelope led me. Unconsciously, I locked the doors on my car as I rode through the dilapidated area until I found

Commerce Street. I slowed my car and looked for door numbers, but most of the houses and apartments barely had doors and windows. Some of the doors were sagging on one hinge; the windows had no screens; and many of the panes were broken and stuffed with newspaper or rags. Paint was virtually nonexistent, and the porches and entrances were crumbling for lack of repair.

I shuttered as I stared at the ruin of the buildings and prayed that I was surely on the wrong street, when I saw a middled-aged lady walking down the street, laden down with a bag of groceries. I pulled up beside her as she headed for one of the apartments.

"Excuse me. But could you tell me if you happen to know where Johnathon Adams lives? He is a little boy with brown hair and big brown eyes, and he is about six..."

"I know who he is, Miss. He lives right beside me, in that house yonder. I don't think ya' want to go over there right now, though. Johnathon's parents' been fighting for about three days now, and with his drinking and all, I wouldn't go in there if it was me."

"I'm Johnathon's teacher from the elementary school, and I just came by to check on him because he has not been in school for the last three days. Do you know if he is all right?"

"I don't rightly know, Ma'am. I ain't seen him myself since Tuesday. I remember 'cause that's the day the cops came out to quieten Johnathon's daddy down a bit. He had really laid one on, I'm here to tell ya'."

"Was Johnathon all right?"

"He was then, Ma'am. I saw him peering through the window, and I waved at him from where I was. I think he's okay. He's a tough little fellow."

"Yes, he is. Well, if you see him, tell him I miss him at school and hope he can return tomorrow."

I turned to leave when a sudden idea came to me.

"You wouldn't, by any chance, be Miss Ada, would you?"

"Well, yes I am! How did ya' know my name?"

"Johnathon talks about you all the time. He really thinks a lot of you and your son."

"Well, ain't that something. You knowing my name and all. If that don't beat all."

"Bye, Miss Ada. Don't forget to tell Johnathon that I've missed him."

I ran to my car and started the engine. As I backed in the muddy ruts to turn around, I brushed at the tears that were quickly forming in the corners of my eyes. Poor little Johnathon! He didn't have a dog's chance to make it in this world!

FIVE

JOHNATHON CAME BACK to school the next day. He was wearing an old, torn jacket that was miles too big for him. When I suggested that he take it off in the classroom, he just shook his head and slouched down in his desk. As the day wore on, the temperature rose to about eighty. Since it was the end of September, the air conditioning had been disconnected, so it didn't take long for the room to become unbearably hot.

When the other children started complaining about the heat, I opened all of the windows and told them to take off all sweaters and jackets, which they shed immediately. All but Johnathon. He remained crouched in his desk, all hunkered down into the dirty, old coat. I walked over to his desk and knelt down beside him. Huge droplets of sweat were running down his brow, and his little face was red as a beet.

"Johnathon, don't you want to take off your jacket now? I know that you would be so much more comfortable without it."

Johnathon slouched down even further in his desk and shook his little head.

"Why, not, Johnthon? It's so hot in here. You have to be burning up in the jacket."

Johnathon didn't answer for a few moments. Then he quietly said, "'Cause."

"Because why, Johnathon? Why would you want to be so hot when taking off the jacket would make you cooler? Here. Let me help you take it off." I reached over and grasped the neck of the jacket, when Johnathon jerked away from me.

"No! No! Leave it alone! I can't take it off!"

"Why, Johnathon, why can't you take it off?"

Johnathon's little eyes filled with tears. "'Cause, Techr, my Daddy said he'd whup me if I took the jacket off today. Please, Techr, don't make me take it off!"

I looked at Johnathon, and a sick feeling of dread filled my stomach. What was Johnathon's dad trying to hide? A rage of fury engulfed me as I grabbed Johnathon's hand and led him to the doorway of my classroom.

"Todd, go and get the principal. Immediately!" As Todd ran from the room, I all but drug Johnathon outside the door into the hall. He was openly crying by then and begging me to let him alone.

"Please, Techr, please! Just let me keep the jacket on! Please, Techr! I don't want no more whuppings! Please,

Techr! Is the princpal goin' to whup me, too? Please, Techr, let me alone!" Johnathon tried to pull away from me, but I held him firmly by the hand.

It seemed like an eternity before Todd reappeared with Mrs. Rice, the principal, following behind him.

"Go back into the classroom, Todd, and finish your seatwork. I'll be back in a minute."

"What's the problem, Mrs. Harris? Is Johnathon acting up again?" Mrs. Rice looked over her glasses at Johnathon, who was hiding behind me by then.

"No, Johnathon has been perfect all morning, Mrs. Rice. But we do seem to have a slight problem that I thought you might need to know. Johnathon's dad told him he could not take off his jacket today, or he would give him a whipping, and it is so hot in the room. Could you help me persuade Johnathon to take off the jacket?"

Using her stern, principal's glare, Mrs. Rice looked Johnathon square in the face and said, "Johnathon, take off the jacket. Now!"

Johnathon dropped his head, sobbing. He slowly let the offending jacket fall to the floor. I stared at him, hoping against hope that my suspicions were not real. But they were. There, hanging from Johnathon's little arm was a dirty rag, tied tightly around the skin. Blood stains dotted the rag through the dirt and grime.

"What is that on your arm, Johnathon?" I knelt down and touched the rag, all the while looking into the face of the most pathetic and tormented little six-year-old that I had ever encountered. "Let me look at your arm, Johnathon." I carefully untied the rag and drew in a quick breath as I stared at an ugly, jagged, swollen cut on the top of Johnathon's little arm.

"It really don't hurt much, Techr. I swear it don't! Please don't tell my Daddy ya' saw it! He'll whup me for sure!"

I stood up and turned away from Johnathon as tears of rage and sorrow consumed me. I didn't have to guess how Johnathon had gotten the cut. I had heard Johnathon tell, too many times, about his father throwing glasses and bottles at him. I felt Mrs. Rice touch me on the shoulder, and when I looked around at her, she just nodded for me to go. But I couldn't leave my Johnathon with her. I had to take care of him myself, because he trusted me for some reason. Pulling myself together, I took Johnathon's hand.

"Well, I'm sure it's not hurting, Johnathon. But I believe that we need to get you a clean bandage. Come on. Let's have the nurse take a look at it and fix it up for you."

We headed down the hall, Johnathon and I, hand in hand. Johnathon's chin hung down to his chest, and I believe that my heart had dropped down into my shoes, for each step that I took felt like I was dragging a ton with me.

I guess anyone who passed us that day probably thought we belonged together. For we both had tear-stained faces, and looks of despair consumed our very beings. Johnathon was worried about another 'whupping.' Me? I was worried about what that father would do to Johnathon when the Department of Social Services got through with him. For I had to report it. It was the law. In order to protect the school, myself, and especially, Johnathon, I had to report it. I had no choice.

SIX

WHEN JOHNATHON didn't show up for school the next day, I panicked. Leaving my class with an aide for a few minutes, I ran to the office to report his absence. The school counselor made a fast call to DSS to get any information she could about what had transpired the previous day after the school had reported Johnathon's cut arm.

"I'm sorry, but we had so many reports yesterday that we had to put the Adams' boy's report on a back docket. But I can assure you that we will get to it as soon as we possibly can. I'm sure that he is in no immediate danger." The social worker rambled on to the counselor about their policies while I paced back and forth, sick with worry for Johnathon.

The counselor finally hung up the phone and turned to face me with disgust. "They didn't do anything! No call, no visit. Nothing!"

I couldn't believe my ears. "Nothing? They let that little boy go back to a drunken father who had nearly cut his arm off with a whiskey bottle, or glass, or something, and they did nothing?"

"Mrs. Harris, a child has to be half dead before these agencies will step in and do something. If you ask me, they're afraid. They're afraid to go into some of the homes, and, afraid of lawsuits."

"So what about poor little Johnathon in the meantime? What happens to him?" I screeched out at the counselor, not because of what she said, but because I felt so helpless just knowing this was an abused child who needed help so desperately.

"I'm sorry, Mrs. Harris. I wish we could do more. I know Johnathon needs help. I've talked to him several times when he was sent to the principal for behavior problems, and I could tell that he had serious complications at home. I've already reported his parents to the authorities on three occasions, but to my knowledge, nothing has been done to this point. I really don't know, legally, what else can be done by the school."

"Well, I know! I may not know all the legalities about child abuse, but I sure as heck know when a child needs someone to fight for him!" Grabbing my purse, I headed out of the office. "Tell Mrs. Rice that I'm going to check on Johnathon. I'll be back in a little while." I headed out of the door of the school when I felt a hand gently touch my shoulder. I turned to see the principal, purse on her shoulder, coming up behind me.

I smiled, weakly, and said in a trembly voice, "Thanks."

"I thought you might need some back-up. Now, show me where your 'favorite' student lives."

A few minutes later, we walked up the crumbling steps of Johnathon's house. Looking around at Mrs. Rice with uncertainty, I knocked on the door. No answer. I knocked again, but to no avail. I could hear a television playing in the background, but no sign of life was heard or seen as we stood there. After what seemed like hours of trying to get someone to the door, we turned and walked back to my car.

I slumped over the steering wheel and rested my head against the coolness of the rubber padding. "I just know he's in there. What can I do?"

"You've done more than any teacher should have to do, Elly. Let's go back to school. You have other students who need you, too, you know."

"I know, Mrs. Rice. And I know that I'm not being fair to them. But they have people who care about them. Johnathon doesn't. I'm all that he has. He trusts me to help him and be here for him. I just can't let him down!"

We rode back to school in silence, both of us sorting through our minds what had happened and knowing in our hearts that little Johnathon Adams was probably in danger. But even I knew that we could not break in the house to see if Johnathon was there.

Mrs. Rice had the police check out the address a little later, but they found nothing unusual to report. With no search warrant, they had to assume that no one was home at the Adams' residence.

I finally trudged back to my classroom on feet that felt like chunks of lead. The day was an eternity for me. I watched the clock and went through the motions of teaching. Thank goodness it was Friday. I really needed a break from the stress Johnathon had put me through that week!

As I headed home for the week-end, my car automatically drove down Commerce Street. I stopped and asked several children who were playing outside if they had seen Johnathon or his parents, but the answer was always the same. Not a soul knew the whereabouts of little Johnathon Adams, or if they did know, they weren't telling.

Finally, I backed my car into the driveway of Johnathon's house and turned around. As I pulled out of the drive, I looked back one last time at Johnathon's house. Suddenly I detected a movement at the window. As I squinted my eyes for better vision, I thought I caught a glimpse of a pair of brown eyes looking through the tattered shade at the window. I slammed on brakes and turned in my seat. But the eyes were gone. I stayed there for a long time, trying to see those eyes again, but they did not reappear while I watched.

On the drive home, I told myself that I probably had imagined seeing that shade move. I also tried to convince myself that I had only pictured, in my mind, those eyes looking at me through the broken panes. But in my heart I knew better. I had become so familiar with those eyes...those big, brown, pleading, sad eyes. Johnathon was there all right….little Johnathon, who loved and trusted me, his 'Techr,' and I just drove away.

SEVEN

THE THING I hated most about teaching was the dreaded bus duty that rolled around much too often to suit me. Yet, when Monday morning arrived, I found myself down at the bus circle, carefully monitoring the arrival of the buses. The teachers who had their regular bus duties that morning eyed me with suspicion when I told them that I would unload bus number nine when it pulled up.

As luck would have it, Johnathon's bus was the last to arrive that crisp, cool Monday morning. By the time I spied it coming near the school, I was almost in a frenzy. My eyes darted quickly down the length of the long, yellow bus until I spotted the little, tousled head at the back of the bus. Johnathon! There he was! My heart gave a huge leap as I clasped my hands and said a silent prayer that Johanthon was all right. About that time, Johnathon saw me, and his face lit up like a Christmas tree. He started waving and grinning from ear to ear, and I could tell that he was mouthing, 'Techr,' even though I couldn't actually hear the words.

The usual hum of childish voices dimmed around me as seventy or more children stepped from the bus. I must have responded to the voices who called out, "Mornin', Miz Harris," although I don't really remember answering. Actually, I barely heard the children talking because my heart was beating so loudly in my ears. It wasn't until I heard, "Techr," that I was able to catch my breath. I looked down at Johnathon who was once again dressed in the dirty, Braves tee shirt and dingy, old jeans, and I could see at a glance that he was okay. My face broke into a smile that I just couldn't control, and I put my arm around Johnathon's little, bony shoulder as we walked side by side to the classroom.

They say that your heart can play funny tricks on you when you're not looking. I don't know about that. I do know that little Johnathon Adams became an obsession with me from that day forward, and I devoted a lot of time to finding out more about him and his pitiful family. I'm afraid it was not a pretty picture.

Through very careful questioning, I found out that the stories Johnathon had told about his father were absolutely true. He was a hopeless alcoholic, often in trouble with the law because of domestic violence during his drunken tirades. He was usually out of work and depended on his wife to support, not only the family, but his expensive alcohol habit.

No one seemed to know much about Johnathon's mother except that she was very young and worked as a waitress in a café downtown. I was told that she had not been on the job too long because the family moved around a lot. Most people didn't even know that Johnathon's mom had two boys and a drunken husband that she supported. She was quiet and kept to herself as she worked night after night on the late shift at the café.

It didn't seem likely that I would be able to get Johnathon's mother or father involved in his school affairs, so I focused my attention on Johnathon. I knew that Johnathon was interested in learning, and in spite of his heredity and environment, I was firmly convinced that, as he had said, "He was a pretty smart boy."

So I went to work. I spent every spare moment that I could find helping Johnathon learn his alphabet and numbers. I helped him everyday during recess time, because he still did not bring in his homework.

It wasn't long before I handed out the first report cards to go home. When Johnathon looked at his grades, his little face fell. "I thought I wuz doin' better, Techr. I been workin' so hard. Why don't I have A's like Todd and Valerie and the others? Why, Techr?"

"Because, Johnathon, you still don't bring in your homework. I can't give you good grades until you start doing your homework. And, Johnathon, don't you want to get to play at recess sometimes? Don't you get tired of always missing your recess?"

Johnathon dropped his little, dirty head and said, softly, "Yes, Ma'am."

"Well, Johnathon, start today to do better. Do you remember what you have for homework today?"

"I 'member, Techr. It wuz to learn a new word that starts with the 'B' sound."

"And don't forget to get your report card signed, Johnathon. Bye, now. I'll see you tomorrow."

"Bye, Techr. I'll have my homework tomorrow. You wait and see. I'll have a new 'B' word." Johnathon ran from the room, knocking people here and there in his excitement to get to the bus. I just let it go. I couldn't change everything overnight.

The next day, bus number nine was late coming in, so I was checking homework when Johnathon came bounding into the room.

"I know, Techr, I know a new 'B' word! I know, Techr!" Johnathon yelled to the top of his lungs as he plopped his bookbag on the floor beside his desk. "Call on me, Techr, I know!" Johnathon ran from his desk to where I was standing in the front of the room and began to tap me on the leg. "Call on me, Techr! I know!"

"Go back to your desk, Johnathon, and raise your hand like everyone else, and I'll call on you." Actually, I was about to burst with excitement because Johnathon Adams had finally done his homework, but I had to make him follow the rules like everyone else.

Johnathon ran back to his desk, but instead of sitting down, he jumped up and down, yelling, "I know, Techr, I know! Call on me, Techr!"

"Johnathon, please sit down and raise your hand quietly. Now, Susan, what is your new 'B' word for today?" Before Susan could answer, Johnathon jumped up again.

"But, Techr, I know a 'B' word! Call on me, Techr. I know!"

"Sit down, Johnathon. Your turn will come. Now, Susan, what is your word?"

Johnathon sat down for about two seconds, then popped up again, waving his arm frantically. "But I know a 'B' word, Techr! Please call on me!"

"Johnathon, sit down and control your voice, and I will call on you. Now, Todd, what is your new 'B' word?"

While Todd was proudly saying the word, *brain*, I heard a loud whisper coming from Johnathon's direction. "I know, Techr! Call on me! I know a 'B' word! Call on me, Techr!"

"Johnathon, please follow the class rules. I'll call on you, but you must obey the rules. Now, Mary Beth, what is your new 'B' word?"

Johnathon sat down, on his hands, this time, and muttered. "You callin' on everybody but me, Techr! I know a 'B' word!"

I couldn't stand it any longer. "Well, Johnathon, what is your new 'B' word?"

Johnathon jumped up beside his desk, put his little hands behind his back like a preacher, and announced, loudly,

"Well, Techr, ya' said we had to learn a brand new word that started with the letter 'B,' and ya' said it can't be *boy,* and it can't be *ball*, and it can't be *bat*. So my new 'B' word is *bit*!"

Thinking that Johnathon was referring to the verb, *bit*, I asked him to explain his new word. "Where did you learn your new 'B' word, Johnathon?"

"Well, Techr, when I went home yesterday, my Mommy wuz home and had her head down on the kitchen table like this." Johnathon put his head down on his folded hands, all the while talking in an excited voice. "So I asked my Mommy, 'Mommy, can you tell me a new word that starts with 'B' so I won't have to stand by the fence tomorrow. Please, Mommy.' But my Mommy said, 'Go on, Johnathon, and don't worry me. I don't feel good.' So, I said, 'Please, Mommy, please just tell me one li'l word that starts with 'B' so I can play with the other kids tomorrow. Please, Mommy!' But my Mommy just looked up at me and shook her head, and that's when I saw her eye, Techr! It wuz all swolled and black, and it wuz mostly closed up, but I ain't s'posed to tell ya' 'bout that. Anyway, Mommy yelled for me to get outta' the kitchen, so I went outside and sat down with my ole dog, George, and thunk real hard. I knew that my li'l brother, Willie, couldn't help me 'cause he still ain't too smart being he still can't talk and all. So the only other person I could ask wuz my Daddy, and he wuz in the bed sick again, Techr, and drankin' that medcin and all. But I just wanted to do my homework so bad, Techr, so's you'd be proud and all, and so's I could go to recess today. So I crept real quiet like in to where my Daddy wuz sleeping, and I said so quiet, 'Daddy, can ya' help me learn a new word that starts with 'B' so I won't have to stand by the fence again, Daddy. I'm so tired of that ole fence, Daddy.' But my daddy just yelled at me and said fo' me to get outta his room 'fore he threw his bottle at me. And, Techr, I sho' didn't want to git hit by that bottle again 'cause it hurts, so I started to back outta Daddy's room, when I heard a loud bamming on the door! And, ya' know what, Techr? The door busted open, and it wuz the poleece come running in. And, Techr, my Mommy jumped up from the table and pointed to her swolled eye, and said, 'He's the one what done this to my eye! He's the one!' And, Techr, she pointed her other finger to where my Daddy wuz on the bed. And, Techr, ya' know what happened?"

Forgetting the other children were listening to this horrible story, I said, "What, Johnathon? What happened?" I just had to know.

"Well, Techr, the poleece come running in my Daddy's room, and they got these shiny thangs and put them on my Daddy's hands, and he couldn't move 'em 'cause it looked like those thangs stuck my Daddy's hands together. And then, Techr, the poleece started dragging my Daddy outta the house, but that's when my Daddy turned 'round and told me a new 'B' word. He said, 'Johnathon, you wanta know a 'B' word? I'll tell you a good one. It's what yo' mama is...she's a bit!' So my new word is *bit*!"

I shook my head and sighed. "Johnathon, sit down, please. You can't use that word."

"But, why, Techr? It's not those words ya' said we can't use. It's a brand new word!"

"Because, Johnathon, it's a bad word that you must not ever say! Now, please sit down in your desk."

Johnathon looked at me with total disbelief on his face, as he eased into his desk. "It can't be no bad word, Techr, 'cause it's what my Mommy is, and she ain't bad!"

"You can't use that word, Johnathon. I'm sorry."

Johnathon began to sob, openly, while the other children looked on in awe. "Please let me use that word, Techr, please. I ain't got no more words to use. Please, Techr. I don't want to have to stand by the fence again or stay in again! Please, Techr!"

For once the other students did not tease or ridicule Johnathon. They just looked, watching like devoted fans, to see what would happen next. I walked back to Johnathon's desk and knelt down beside him. "I'll help you with a new word that starts with 'B', Johnathon. Look at me, Johnathon. I'll help you."

Johnathon raised his tearstained face and looked me directly in the eye. "You'll help me, Techr? You'll help me have a new 'B' word so I won't have to stand by the fence today?"

"Yes, Johnathon, I'll help you, and you will not have to stay in or stand by the fence today. No, sir! You will go to recess today!" I gently put my hand on Johnathon's little, trembling shoulder. Now about that word. How about...*brave*."

Johnathon didn't respond, but looked at my hand, resting on his shoulder. He leaned his dirty little head into my hand and looked up shyly at me. "You know som'em,' Techr? I like it when ya' put your hand on my shoulder like that. It makes me feel all warm like." Then Johnathon leaned over toward me and sniffed. "Techr, you know som'em else? You smell just about as good as my ole hound dog!"

The other children laughed, thinking Johnathon had really offended me this time. But I had just received the best compliment I could ever hope to get. Johnathon had placed me in the category with the only thing in the world who loved him...his old dog, and I was mighty happy to share places with old 'George,' in Johnathon's heart.

"Wanna sit with me, Techr? I'll make room so's ya' can help me with my new word." Johnathon scooted over in his desk, and I scrunched in beside him. As I started to write the word, *brave*, on Johnathon's tablet, he looked up at me. He motioned for me to lean down. "Techr, do ya' have a little boy?"

I shook my head, as I watched Johnathon's face light up.

Motioning for me to lean down again, Johnathon whispered, "Well, Techr, if ya' ever git to wantin' a little boy real bad, could I be yo' little boy sometimes?"

With a huge lump in my throat, I smiled at this precious little soul, and nodded. The tousled head leaned against me again, and those eyes..those endearing brown eyes held me in a trance as two scrawny arms hugged me tightly. "I love you, Techr!"

Johnathon went to recess that day and everyday after that. I helped him with his homework before he went home each day, and his grades soared. His next report card looked like Todd's and Mary Ellen's and Valerie's. Except for one thing...his report cards were never signed.

EIGHT

THE YEAR WITH JOHNATHON clipped on at an alarming rate, and it wasn't long before the cool, crisp days of Autumn were upon us. By that time, all of my students were reading, even Johnathon. Actually, if the truth were known, Johnathon was probably the best reader in my class, and he knew it, too. He constantly yelled out the words when another child faltered, so I finally just had to bend some of the rules for Johnathon. I did try to channel some of his enthusiasm toward helping other students at their desks, but, more often than not, a fuss resulted when Johnathon tried to copy "Techr," too much, and I had to intervene.

But, all in all, Johnathon gained a new respect from the other children with his new-found knowledge and abilities, and they started to include him in their play activities as well. Johnathon blossomed with the attention, and I was overjoyed that maybe, just maybe, I was making a difference in little Johnathon's life.

Then, a new student was placed in my classroom. Patrick Martin. He came on Columbus Day, October 12th. I guess I remember the exact day because twenty minutes after Patrick walked into the room, he proceeded to tell the class, in great detail, all about Columbus, and why it was a special day. I listened, dumbfounded. This child was nothing short of brilliant. He was also handsome, dressed in the latest styles, and the only son of a board member. And, Johnathon hated him, immediately!

When lunch time came around, most of the class begged me to let them sit with Patrick. They scurried quickly to get in line beside him, and all vied for his attention. All, but Johnathon. He just sat in his desk when I called his row to line up, and, only, reluctantly, walked to the end of the line when I insisted that he join the rest of the class.

Johnathon sat at my table during lunch and watched the reaction of the class to Patrick. He picked at his food, which, in itself, was unusual, because he always cleaned his plate in record time.

"Are you feeling all right, Johnathon? You haven't touched your lunch." I leaned over to feel Johnathon's head to see if he had a fever. Johnathon pulled away from my hand with a shrug.

"I ain't got no fever, Techr. I jest ain't hungry, that's all." My eyes followed Johnathon's stare to the first table where Patrick Martin had the other students enthralled.

"Patrick seems to be a very nice boy, don't you think, Johnathon?"

"I guess, Techr. If ya' like the sissy type and all. I don't much care for that yeller hair and blue eyes on a boy. Do you, Techr?"

"Oh, I think Patrick is very nice-looking, Johnathon. It really doesn't matter how people look, though, if they are good people inside."

"Todd and the others like him better than me now. Well, I don't like him a bit! He's jest a sissy, that's all!" Johnathon slid down in his chair, crossed his arms over his chest, and frowned.

"Johnathon, don't say ugly things about Patrick. Why, you don't even know him yet. And I'm sure that the other children still like you, Johnathon. It's just that Patrick's new to the class."

Johnathon shrugged and didn't say anymore throughout the lunch period. Actually, Johnathon was about the quietest I had ever seen him for the rest of the day. He stayed close to me during recess and just watched Patrick. When we went inside, Johnathon went straight to his desk without having to be reminded. There, he continued his vigil, watching the new boy with a sadness that seemed to consume him. At the sound of the final bell, Johnathon quietly packed his bookbag and left to catch his bus. It was the first time all year that he had not told me good bye.

The next day, Patrick came into the room right as the last bell rang. He was sporting a brand new bookbag on his back, and carried what looked like a very small, brown, paper bag in his hand.

"Good morning, Patrick. I changed some seats around this morning, and you will now be sitting on the third row, right next to Johnathon. I hope you'll like your new desk. If you have any questions, I'm sure that Johnathon will be more than glad to help you out." I crossed my fingers and silently prayed that this move would help Johnathon become friends with Patrick.

Patrick went to his new desk and smiled politely. "I'm sure I will like it just fine, Mrs. Harris. Thank you."

Johnathon seethed and shot me piercing looks from those big, brown eyes of his. I looked him straight in the face, and, without saying a word, let him know that I expected him to be nice or else. What I didn't see was the sneer that Patrick gave to Johnathon when I turned my back. Nor did I see the many times during the morning when Patrick reached into his desk and snacked on the various pieces of candy that he had brought to school in the little, tiny, brown, paper bag. But Johnathon did. He saw it all and said nothing.

Day after day, Patrick entered the room with the little, paper bag, and day after day, Johnathon watched him sneak his candy when I wasn't looking. I did notice that Johnathon and Patrick never became friends, but since things were relatively calm, I didn't worry too much about it. Little did I know that Johnathon was busy formulating a plan of his own as he watched Patrick sneak candy everyday without my knowledge.

One morning, around the first of November, just when the days were starting to get cold with a hint of winter in the air, Johnathon came walking in the classroom, wearing a huge, purple jacket that had to belong to some adult. The jacket was bulging around the middle, and he held it together with his hands. The other children laughed when they saw him, but he just walked past them and headed for his desk.

I didn't notice when Johnathon took off his jacket, but he did appear to be about thirty pounds lighter when the ugly, purple thing ended up in a pile under his desk. I turned around to write the new vocabulary words on the board, when I heard paper rattling. I looked back to see what it was, but everyone was busily practicing their handwriting, and nothing seemed to be amiss. I thought that maybe I had imagined the paper rattling, so I went back to my task at the board. There it was again. I heard paper rattling, louder this time.

"Who is rattling paper?" I looked from child to child, but everyone seemed innocent of the accusation. When I looked at Johnathon, he was all bent over his paper, writing his letters with a fervor. I turned back to the board, only to hear the rattling once again, and a sort of munching in addition. Either we had a huge rat in the room, or I was hearing things. I decided to investigate.

Pretending to look over some papers, I nonchalantly walked around the room, listening intently for the rustling, crunching noise. There it was again! Never taking my eyes from the papers in my hands, I eased over to where the noise was the loudest. I found myself standing right next to Johnathon's desk. At a glance, I could tell that I had caught the culprit. Johnathon was leaning over his desk with his left hand inside the ugly, purple jacket under his desk. Sensing that I was standing beside him, he slowly looked up. If I hadn't known better, I would have thought that he had a severe case of the mumps from the way his cheeks were protruding. Putting my hands on my hips, I stood to one side and began tapping my foot.

"What are you doing, Johnathon? What's under your coat? And what do you have in your mouth?"

Johnathon struggled to answer, but his mouth was so full that he nearly choked.

"Go and get a drink of water at the sink, Johnathon. Then, I want you to show me what you have under that jacket."

Johnathon had everyone's attention as he trudged to get a drink of water. When he returned to his desk, I was still waiting for him. "Show me, Johnathon. What is under your jacket?"

As if in slow motion, Johnathon reluctantly picked up the purple jacket. Under it was a huge, grocery bag filled with broken, saltine crackers, potato chips, stale bread, and various other items of food that I didn't recognize. After examining the bag, I was very puzzled. Johnathon knew better than to bring food to school. He certainly knew it was against the rules to eat in the classroom.

"Johnathon, please go outside the room and wait for me in the hall." I had to know why Johnathon had deliberately disobeyed school rules when he had been doing so much better.

Approaching Johnathon outside the room, I shook my head. "Why, Johnathon? Why did you bring all of that...that...stuff to school in a big grocery bag? And then sit in class and eat it right under my nose. Why, Johnathon?"

The tears were already falling from Johnathon's eyes when I knelt down and took his little trembling shoulders in my hands. "Why, Johnathon? Tell me."

"'Cause, Techr, I wanted to be like Patrick. 'Cept I didn't have no li'l, bitty bags like his, and I didn't have no candy at my house neither. So I jest brought what I had. That wuz the only bag I could find. It come from the Piggly Wiggly store. Please, Techr, I wuz jest trying to do what Patrick does, and he don't never git caught!"

As I listened to Johnathon's explanation, my heart just overflowed with love. Who else but Johnathon would have thought to bring a great, big grocery bag filled with Lord knows what to school? And have the gall to sit in class and eat away at the mixed-up concoction? Only Johnathon, that's who! Suddenly I knew what I had to do.

"Well, Johnathon, I'm really glad that you brought that bag to school. I need one to carry some things home in, and I believe that the one you brought is just the right size. Can I have it?"

Johnathon stopped crying and looked at me in disbelief. "Yes, Ma'am, Techr. You sure can have it. You sure can!"

"Well, go on back into the room now, Johnathon, and put your jacket back over the bag. I'll get it when I'm ready to leave this afternoon. Oh, by the way, Johnathon.

Don't eat any more of the...uh...goodies that you have in the bag. It'll spoil your lunch."

"Oh, don't worry, Techr. I ain't goin' to eat no more o' my stuff 'cause I'm goin' to give it to you! You can eat it for your lunch instead o' that ole salad ya' eat everyday."

"Well, thank you, Johnathon. What a treat! Now go back inside and get your writing assignment finished." As I watched that proud, little fellow skip back into the room, I sighed, then doubled over in laughter. Johnathon and his big, old, grocery sack full of crumbled, stale, sickening, food scraps! And he wanted me to eat his treasure for lunch? In no way would I eat that mess!

But I did. When we went to the cafeteria that day, I was busy seating the class when Johnathon came up behind me and tapped me on the leg.

"Techr, you fergot som'em." At a glance I could see that Johnathon had the unsightly, brown, grocery bag behind his back, as if it were some great surprise. Some surprise! I inwardly groaned as Johnathon brought the sack around in front of him. "You forgot your special lunch, Techr! But I 'membered! And I'll sit with ya' so's I can watch ya' eat that good ole lunch!"

Well, Johnathon was true to his word. He sat right beside me and watched intently as I ate the crumbled saltines, the stale potato chips, the dried, hard, peanut butter sandwich, and something else that I could never identify.

I missed school the next day. It was the only day that I had missed in all my years of teaching, and it was because of Johnathon. I was sick! Everything that I had eaten from

Johnathon's precious, grocery sack ended up coming out of me from one end or the other, and it took me about twenty-four hours to get my stomach settled down.

Johnathon offered to bring me food many times after that, but I told him that the doctor had put me on a very strict diet, and I could only eat certain things. I hope the good Lord understood why I lied.

Patrick certainly never understood how I found out about his little sack of candy that he inhaled each day. I saw a new side to Patrick when I told him he could not bring anymore candy to school. I guess maybe I saw the same, ostentatious child who annoyed Johnathon so much. Johnathon once told Patrick that he acted just like Nellie Olsen on "Little House on the Prairie," and I do believe that he was right! When I thought back to it, I remembered that Nellie Olsen's mother had been a school board member, too.

I moved Patrick to the front of the room after the grocery bag incident. Johnathon thought that I had moved Patrick so I could watch for his little bags of candy. But he was wrong. I really moved him so that Johnathon could have some peace again and be his own person.

So Johnathon settled down, worked hard again, and let his envy of Patrick become a thing of the past. All went well for about two weeks.

NINE

JUST BEFORE THANKSGIVING HOLIDAYS, I noticed a change in Johnathon. For one thing, he stopped riding the bus to school. When I quizzed him about how he was getting to school, he just raised his shoulders and didn't answer. So I had another teacher watch for me. She reported that Johnathon was riding with a man in an old, beat-up, Ford Taurus.

So I approached Johnathon again. "Who's the man bringing you to school, Johnathon? Is your Dad out of jail?"

"No, Ma'am, Daddy's still in jail, and his name is Jack." Johnathon walked to his desk and didn't explain any further. But he was different. The usual, chatty Johnathon was sullen and quiet. He had little to say to the other children or to me. He just kept to himself, did his work, and put his head down on his desk when he finished an assignment.

I worried a lot about Johnathon that week, and I was plenty curious as to this Jack fellow. I figured he must be

"Mommy's" new boyfriend, but I wasn't sure. Since I didn't notice any marks or cuts on Johnathon, I tried to put it out of my mind.

We got busy with Thanksgiving activities that week, and all of the children seemed to be excited about the upcoming holidays, except for Johnathon. When the other students made place mats to take home for their big, Thanksgiving dinners, Johnathon just put his head down. I figured that Johnathon wasn't interested in the place mats because he didn't anticipate a big turkey and dressing dinner at his house. So I let him watch and do nothing.

When everyone drew turkeys, pilgrims and Indians, Johnathon tore up his papers. He didn't say a word as he walked to the trash can and dropped in the ruined drawings.

"Why did you do that, Johnathon? I thought your drawings were very good." I tried to get this troubled, little boy to talk to me. "Is something wrong, Johnathon?"

"I jest didn't like 'em, that's all, Techr." Johnathon dropped his head back to his desk and stared across the room. I finally decided that he just didn't feel well, and so I went on with the activities for the day.

When the final bell rang that day, Johnathon slowly got up from his desk and walked out to where the car riders loaded to go home. I watched him through the window. He walked slowly to the old Ford and got in the back seat. I could tell that a man was driving, but I couldn't make out who was sitting in the front seat next to him. It looked like a woman, probably Johnathon's mother, although I couldn't be sure. I watched as the car sped away from the school, screeching tires as it left.

The attendance clerk at the school looked up from her work, when I walked into her office.

"Can you check on something for me, Kathy? I've noticed that Johnathon Adams has been riding to school in a car this week. I just wondered if you had an address change on him." I sat down in a chair next to Kathy's desk while she looked up the statistics for my class on her computer.

"You know, it seems like I did have an address change on someone from your class this past Monday. Let me see who it was." Kathy scrolled down the names until she came to Adams. "His address is listed as 214 Bunker Road. Is that where he has always lived?"

"No, he was living on Commerce Street. I know because I've been by there several times. I wonder why he moved?"

"I don't remember who called about the change of address. Wish I could help you more, Elly. I just don't remember. I have so many people coming in and out."

"That's all right, Kathy. I appreciate you looking up the address for me. If you get any more changes on Johnathon, could you let me know? I really worry about that child."

"Sure thing, Elly. Sorry I couldn't help you more."

As I walked back to my room, I couldn't get Johnathon out of my mind. Maybe it was the move to a new place that had caused a change in him. He was acting very strange. With a promise to myself to check out Johnathon's new address over the holidays, I went back to my work.

The next day was the last day of school prior to Thanksgiving break, and I had a lot of preparations to do before the children came to school. I had planned a re-enactment of the first Thanksgiving, and all of the children were going to dress like either Indians or Pilgrims. Well, actually, they were only going to wear headdresses or feathers, except for Todd, who was going to be dressed in his Dad's authentic Indian costume that he had made during his scouting days, and Patrick, of course, who was wearing an expensive Pilgrim outfit his Mother had ordered from Macy's.

Johnathon's problems easily slipped from my mind as I scurried from place to place that afternoon, gathering "authentic" food items that the children would feast on the next day.

I'm sorry to say that I really didn't notice Johnathon when he entered the room the following day. He must have slipped into his desk when I was gluing feathers to the Indian headbands. About midmorning, when I took the headbands around to the students, I did notice that Johnathon was sitting quietly in his desk with his head down.

"Here's your headband, Johnathon. I thought you would like to be an Indian today." Johnathon reached out and took the headband, but said nothing. He just laid it on his desk and put his head back down. I was about to ask Johnathon if he felt all right when a commotion broke out on the other side of the room, and I had to deal with that.

As the day wore on, I felt totally drained. The excitement of the children and the holiday activities wore me down, both physically and mentally. I was really glad when the bell rang to signify that the Thanksgiving break had finally arrived.

The children literally ran out of the room, talking louder than usual in their frenzy to get home. I walked down the hall with them to make sure they all got to the bus room or in their cars safely. That was when I noticed Johnathon. He walked slowly down the steps of the school and out to the street where the cars were loading. He paused at the street, with his little feet pigeon-toed, and watched the long line of cars as they stopped near the crossing guard. I supposed he was looking for the old, Ford Taurus that he had been riding in for the past week.

Johnathon just stood there for a while, holding his Indian headband in his little hand and looking at the line of cars in the drive. I watched that sad little boy who had stolen my heart and felt a pang of guilt that I had not spent more time with him that day.

Suddenly, without warning, Johnathon started running after one of the cars. He bolted straight down the street, yelling at the top of his lungs.

"Wait! Wait! I need to go home with you! Wait!"

I'm not sure who ran the fastest, the crossing guard or me. We both took off after Johnathon as fast as we could. Maybe it was the adrenaline that was pumping in my veins, I don't know, but I managed to pass the officer and caught Johnathon just as he approached the first intersection near the school. I grabbed him by the arm and swung him around to face me.

"Johnathon! For Heavens' sake! What are you doing, running down the road like that? Don't you know that a car could easily have hit you?"

Tears streamed down Johnathon's face as he tried to pull out of my grasp.

"Let me go, Techr! I gotta catch that car! Let me go!"

I held on even tighter to Johnathon as he struggled against me. "No, Johnathon! Stop pulling against me!" Johnathon started sobbing loudly as I took his shaking, little body into my arms. "Come on with me, Honey. Let's walk back to the school and find out what's wrong."

Johnathon felt like dead weight, leaning against me as we walked back down the street and up the steps to the school. I knew I had to have help with this one, so we headed straight for the principal's office. Johnathon stayed right by my side, pressing into my leg and crying quietly.

Mrs. Rice saw the two of us coming, shook her head from side to side, and moved back so that we could enter her office. I sat down on her couch, and, with my arm firmly around Johnathon, I proceeded to tell the principal what had just happened.

"Why were you chasing the car, Johnathon?" Mrs. Rice pulled up a chair and got on the level with Johnathon as she quizzed him. Johnathon didn't answer. He just continued to cry with his little head drooping to his shoulders.

I reached around and took Johnathon's tear-stained face in my hands. "It's all right, Johnathon. We just want to help you. Tell Mrs. Rice who was in the car that you were chasing. Was it Jack?"

Johnathon looked up at me and shook his head. "It wudden Jack, Techr. I thank it wuz some folks who lived near me at the other place cross town. It looked like they car."

"But why were you chasing their car, Johnathon? Isn't Jack coming for you today?" I looked up at my principal, and she rolled her eyes back in her head. She was as puzzled as I was with Johnathon's answer.

Johnathon dropped his head. "Jack said he ain't comin' today, Techr. So I wuz trying to find somebody else to go home with."

"Why isn't Jack coming today, Johnathon? Don't you live with him now?" I assumed that he and his mom had moved in with Jack.

"I can't live wid' Jack no more, Techr, not after what happened last night."

"What happened, Johnathon?" Mrs. Rice and I chorused in together.

Johnathon fidgeted with his bookbag before he answered. "Well, last night the poleece come to Jack's place, and they took my Mommy jest like they took my Daddy, Techr. And they took li'l Willie, too, 'cause my Mommy was feedin' him with her titties. I don't know why they come... and... and... took my Mommy and Willie, Techr, but...but... they did, 'cause I wuz hiding behind the door, and I saw 'em." Johnathon started to sob again as he relayed the heartbreaking story. "Techr, I bet my Mommy and li'l Willie don't come home no more jest like my Daddy didn't. And...and...Jack said I can't live wid' him no more!"

I closed my eyes and blinked back the tears that were threatening to spill any moment. Mrs. Rice took over for me and continued to question Johnathon.

"Tell us exactly what Jack told you, Johnathon."

Johnathon looked up at me, and I nodded at him to tell the principal.

"It's all right, Johnathon. Tell Mrs. Rice and me what Jack told you."

"Okay, Techr. Well, when Jack brought me to school this morning, he...he... said for me to find somewhere else to live today, 'cause I sure as Hell couldn't live wid' him no more." Johnathon quickly clamped his hands over his mouth. "I'm sorry, Techr, I didn't mean to say that bad word, but that's what Jack said."

I couldn't believe what I heard. That sorry, low-down creep, that Jack, whoever he was, had put this little six-year-old child out at school, and told him to find himself another place to live. And then he just disappeared! So that was why Johnathon had been chasing a car down the street. He needed someone to take him home, for he had no place to go.

I looked at this precious child, who was so burdened down with problems at the tender age of six, and I just openly cried. Johnathon reached up and brushed a tear from my face with his grubby, little finger.

"Don't cry, Techr. It'll be all right. Don't cry."

"But, Johnathon, why didn't you tell me you had no where to go this afternoon? Why, Johnathon? You know I would have helped you."

"'Cause you wuz so busy makin' headbands and all, Techr. You didn't have time to worry 'bout me. 'Sides, I figgered I'd see somebody I know who wouldn't mind me goin' home wid' em 'fore the day wuz over."

"Oh, Johnathon!" I reached over and lifted Johnathon on my lap, and we just hugged each other and cried. Johnathon had a weight heavier than life to bear, and "Techr," well, I had a weight of guilt that threatened to rip my heart right out of my body.

When I came to my senses, I realized that Mrs. Rice was talking on the telephone with Social Services. After explaining Johnathon's situation to them, she listened intently for a few minutes.

"What?" she screamed. "I can't believe what I'm hearing! Call the police! But you're the agency that handles abandoned children, are you not?"

After holding the receiver for a few seconds more, the principal slammed down the phone and turned to me.

"Johnathon, please go and sit in the outer office for a minute. I need to talk to your teacher."

Johnathon looked frantically at me. "It's all right, Johnathon. I'm not going anywhere. I will not leave you. Don't worry. Just do what Mrs. Rice asked you to do."

Johnathon reluctantly walked out of the principal's office and sat in a chair near the secretary. I looked back to Mrs. Rice. "What did they say?"

"They said that this was a police problem, and that they could not do anything until the police took Johnathon into custody."

"The police will scare Johnathon to death! He's watched both his mother and his father get hauled away to jail by the police, and he'll be so frightened if we have to call them. Mrs. Rice, I have an idea. Can I take Johnathon home with me, just for the holidays? I'd really like to, if it's okay."

"Elly, I'd better check with the police first. If they say it's okay, then it's all right with me. I'd say that what Johnathon needs most, right now, is someone to love him."

But it seemed that the police had rules and guidelines to follow, and they wouldn't let a child go home with someone who was not a registered foster parent. And, so, we were back to square one. Johnathon had nowhere to go. The authorities didn't want him, but they wouldn't let the only person in the world who loved the little fellow take him home.

After numerous phone calls back and forth to Social Services and the police station, two huge, uniformed officers strolled into the school. It was about five o'clock in the afternoon, and Johnathon was still sitting in the little chair beside the secretary's desk. He wasn't crying anymore. He didn't talk, and he didn't fidget. He just sat there and stared off in space.

I couldn't look at him. It just broke my heart all over again everytime I glanced his way.

When the two policemen walked up to Johnathon, he turned his head, got up quietly, and walked away with them. If he had looked back, he would have seen his teacher and his principal crumpled together, sobbing uncontrollably. But he never looked back.

TEN

I WENT THROUGH THE MOTIONS of preparing for Thanksgiving that year. I baked a twenty pound turkey, made the dressing just like my Mama had taught me to do with good old southern cornbread as the base, and remembered to get "cranberry sauce shaped like the can" for my brother, Ted. I baked sweet potato pies and even found the time to make my Dad a great, big coconut cake. My entire family gathered round on Thursday to give thanks for another year and to eat the feast I had prepared.

Everything must have tasted good, for there was very little left at the end of the day. But I really don't remember eating anything. After dinner, my husband took my hand and led me to the peaceful backyard, away from the noise and activity in the house.

"What's wrong, Elly? You've been so quiet, and you hardly touched that delicious meal. Tell me what's wrong."

"Oh, Will! It's little Johnathon again! I can't seem to get him off my mind." I burst into tears as my ever-patient husband of five years put his strong arm around my trembling shoulders and led me to the wooden swing under the big, oak tree. I sniffled loudly as I snuggled into the protection of his comforting arm, and I relayed the painful story of what had happened to Johnathon on the day before Thanksgiving break. A fresh, torrent of tears started anew as I finished the story.

"Will. You cannot imagine how his little face looked when the policemen took him off down that hall. He had trusted me, Will! I was his hope and his comfort, and he trusted me to look after him, and I let him down!" I sobbed openly as my sadness passed to my loving and caring husband.

"Have you tried to call and find out where he is now? Surely they'll tell you that."

"Yes, I did call, about fifty times, but I keep getting put off because I am not a 'Blood Relative.' Trust me, Will, I don't think Johnathon could handle anymore 'Blood Relatives!' They all seem to end up in jail!"

"Did you try contacting the Department of Social Services?"

"Would you believe, Will, that they're closed for the holidays? I guess I'll have to try to endure the time until I can get back to school and find out what has happened to my Johnathon. I just wish Monday would hurry up and get here!"

"You know, Elly, I believe that this is the first time I can ever remember you wanting your holidays to hurry and end. I'm beginning to think that you've really fallen in love with 'this other man in your life.' Have you, Elly? Have you fallen in love with Johnathon?"

"Oh, yes, Will! I love that little boy just like he was my own son. I have trouble understanding how God could give those sorry parents a son like Johnathon, when we would have been such good parents, Will, and we'll never be able to have children. Oh, yes, I DO wish Johnathon was my son. But he's not, and I may never see him again!"

But I did. On Monday morning, Johnathon walked back into my classroom and looked up at me with those big, brown eyes. He was wearing the old, Braves tee shirt and the baggy jeans, but they did look a little cleaner than usual.

"Hey, Techr. You sure do look purty today. I don't live with Jack no more and not my Mommy, neither, 'cause she's still in jail. But ya' know something, Techr? The poleece didn't put me in jail! They give me ice cream and those chawclate cookies with the white stuff in the middle, and they said they wuz goin' to git me a place to stay while my Mommy wuz in jail, and they did, too! And ya' know what, Techr! I had turkey and cake and everything good to eat for Thanksgiving. Did you git to eat turkey, Techr? 'Cause if ya' didn't, I brot you some!"

Johnathon dropped his bookbag and started digging inside. In just a few seconds he brought out a small bag, crammed full of turkey.

"Miz Binson, that's the lady I'm staying wid' now, she said I could take ya' some turkey, beings we had so much left over and all. I told her that ya' don't never have much to eat and how nice ya' are and all, Techr."

"Oh, Johnathon!" I stooped down, took the package of turkey in one hand and reached my arms around that little boy and hugged him with all my might. "Oh, thank you, Johnathon. No, I don't remember eating any turkey. What a treat! Thank you, Johnathon! You have made my day!"

Johnathon grinned from ear to ear as he walked back to his desk. He thought the gift of the turkey had made me so happy. He never knew it was the gift of having another chance with the boy that had filled my day with Thanksgiving.

I found out later that Johnathon had been placed in a foster home by social services until the mother was released from jail. So for about three weeks, Johnathon came to school clean, apparently well-fed, and seemingly happy. He chattered incessantly about his new "family," and I really thought that maybe Johnathon might have a chance after all.

That was the three weeks before Christmas break. Everyday Johnathon came to school with his homework, and he was literally high on life. He eagerly tackled every assignment, and the other children started warming up to him again.

Then, without warning, Johnathon's mother was released from jail so that she could "look after" her children. It was exactly two days before the Christmas holidays, and Johnathon was once again ripped from his surroundings to go back to live with his mother and little brother, Willie.

The fact that this "mother" had written twenty, bad checks did not seem to factor into the judge's decision to release her from jail. Nor did the fact that Johnathon was happy for the first time since I had met him. The judge thought Johnathon needed to be with his "real" mother during the holidays. But I feared that this was one time a judge made a bad decision. And I was right! I remember that right after the Christmas holidays, little Johnathon had the toughest time of all!

ELEVEN

THE FIRST DAY OF SCHOOL after the two week Christmas break brought chattering children donned in all sorts of new clothes back into the school room. They were all carrying toys of different sorts to share with their classmates during "Show and Tell" time at the beginning of the day. I let the excitement of the Christmas spirit go on for a while, when it suddenly dawned on me that Johnathon was not in the room. I walked to the door and looked outside in the hallway. There he stood, in his old clothes, kicking at some imaginary piece of dust on the floor with those worn, oversized sneakers, untied as usual.

"Johnathon, aren't you coming into the room today? Everybody's in there having so much fun telling about their Christmas toys and what all they did during the holidays. Come on in the room now and join in the fun before we have to get down to our work for today."

Johnathon continued to look down and kick at the floor tile. The tattered, dingy shoelaces of the old, hand-me-down shoes flopped back and forth as his foot scraped across the floor. I reached over and touched his arm. He jerked away from my touch with a vengeance and stormed into the classroom.

"Okay! I'm going! I don't see what everybody's so excited about! Christmas is stupid, and all this stuff they brought to school is stupid, too! It's jest plain stupid!" Johnathon kicked at the floor as he made his way across the room to his desk.

"Hey, Johnathon! How do you like my new football that I got from Santa Claus?" Todd asked loudly as Johnathon passed by his desk.

"It's stupid, just like you are, that's what! It's stupid,and Christmas is stupid! So shut up, Todd, and get that stupid ball outta my face!"

"Johnathon! Apologize to Todd immediately! What is the matter with you this morning?" I glared at Johnathon as I stood near his desk, tapping my foot, with my hands firmly placed on my hips.

"Okay. I'm sorry! I'm sorry, so there! But Christmas is stupid and so is that stupid game! And get that stupid doll outta my face, Kathy! It has a stupid face, just like yours!"

Kathy started bawling, and Johnathon sneered at her. His tongue came darting out of his mouth as he added to Kathy's misery over her doll.

"Johnathon! What is wrong with you? Kathy's doll is perfectly beautiful, and you know it! Tell her you're sorry for being mean to her this instant!" I leaned over

Johnathon's desk as I demanded an apology from him. He jumped backwards, kicked over the desk, and yelled out.

"I'm sorry, Techr! I'm sorry I wuz mean! I jest don't know why they had to bring all this stupid stuff to school today! It's all stupid, and Christmas is stupid, and I don't like Christmas, and I jest don't see why they all had to bring all those stupid thangs to school!" Johnathon had tears streaming down his little face by the time he finished his loud tirade against Christmas.

"Johnathon! Pick up your desk and have a seat, young man! I am disappointed in you! And tell everyone that you are sorry for the way you have acted this morning! Now!"

Johnathon slowly walked back to his desk and placed it upright, while the rest of the children watched in total amazement. He sat down, reluctantly, and put his head on his desk. A very weak, 'I'm sorry,' came from his trembling lips as the tears continued to flow from his big, brown eyes.

Before I could stop her, Valerie asked, "So, what did you bring for 'Show and Tell,' Johnathon?"

"I didn't bring nuttin', so shut up, Valerie! And get that stupid, crying doll outta my sight!"

"Johnathon! Stop it immediately! Class, it's time for you to go outside for recess. Line up at the door, and Mrs. Brown will watch you. Johnathon, you stay in with me!"

Johnathon jumped up from his desk, clasping his grubby, little hands together. "Please, Techr! Don't make me stay in! I'm sorry for those thangs I said! Please, Techr! Please let me go out! I promise I'll be good! Please, Techr!"

"No, Johnathon! We are going to have a talk while the other children are playing. You stay in your desk."

Johnathon's tears came pouring out of his pitiful eyes as he continued to beg. "Please, Techr! I'm sorry. Please let me go! I won't be mean no more! Please!"

I shook my head from side to side as the last of the other children filed from the room, leaving me alone with a loudly, weeping Johnathon. I pulled up a chair, close to Johnathon's desk, and calmly started to question him. "Why, Johnathon, why don't you like Christmas?"

"I jest don't like it, Techr," Johnathon sobbed. "It's jest a stupid ole holiday, and I don't like it!"

"Why do you think it's stupid, Johnathon? You were all excited about Christmas before we got out of school two weeks ago."

Johnathon slowly brought his little, tear-stained face up from his desk and looked at me with the saddest eyes I believe that I have ever seen. "I jest don't like Christmas, Techr. I hope it don't never come agin!"

I took Johnathon's little face in my hands and looked at him. "Tell, me, Johnathon. Why do you hate Christmas so? And why didn't you bring something that you got for Christmas to school today to share with the other children? Did you forget?"

"Techr, I didn't forgit. I didn't bring nuttin' to school today 'cause I didn't git nuttin' fo' Christmas!" A new flood of tears streamed down Johnathon's face as he started to tell about his Christmas holidays. "Techr, I wuz excited 'bout Christmas when I went home for the holidays. But my Mommy wudden' feeling so good and didn't want me and li'l Willie to make much fuss 'bout Christmas much. So me and li'l Willie, we jest waited and hoped that Santa Claus would come to bring us som'em. On the day before Christmas, I went in my Mommy's room where she wuz restin' and asked her if she reckoned Santa would brang me and li'l Willie jest one li'l present, and Mommy said, 'Get outta here and quit worring me, Johnathon! Ain't no Santa Claus comin' to this house Now go on outta my room and let me rest.' And I said, ' But, Mommy, don't Santa Claus go to everybody's house and take children presents?' But Mommy said, 'Ain't no Santa Claus comin' to this house!' So I asked Mommy if we could git a li'l Christmas tree, then, so it would seem like Christmas. But Mommy said that she couldn't 'ford no tree and to git outta her room 'fore she slapped me agin."

"Techr, I took li'l Willie outta Mama's room then, and I put him to bed. I told li'l Willie not to worry 'cause I wuz goin' to pray fo' Santa Claus to come. And I did, Techr! I knelt down sides my bed that night 'fore Christmas, Techr, and I said, 'Dear God, please help Santa Claus to find our house tonight and brang li'l Willie and me jest one li'l present. And, God, can ya' have him brang jest a real, li'l Christmas tree, too. And, God, I'm going to try to be so good. Amen.' Then I got in my bed sides Willie, Techr, and I jest knew that God would make Santa Claus come to see Willie and me."

By that time the tears were falling from my eyes as hard as Johnathon's were. I walked over to my desk and got some tissues, and we both blew our noses loudly as Johnathon continued his story.

"What happened on Christmas Day, Johnathon? Did you ever get a Christmas tree?" I knew the answer before Johnathon had a chance to reply.

"No, Ma'am, Techr. I guess God wuz too busy on that night 'fore Christmas to listen to me. When me and li'l Willie woke up on Christmas mornin,' there wudden' no tree, and there wudden' no present for li'l Willie and me. The house wuz cold and jest the same as it wuz the night before. I told li'l Willie didn't nobody love us, not even Santa Claus, but I don't think li'l Willie unnerstood, Techr. He wuz jest hungry. So I went in the kitchen and found some peanut butter and put it on some ole bread and give it to li'l Willie, and he seemed to be happy wid it. I told Willie agin that didn't nobody love us, when ya' know what, Techr? Ya' know what I 'membered all of a sudden? I did have som'em that loved me. It wuz my ole hound dog, George. George loved me, Techr, so I 'cided to go outside and play with ole George on Christmas Day."

I watched Johnathon's sad, brown eyes fill with fresh tears as I listened to perhaps the most tragic Christmas story ever told in a first grade classroom.

"Did you play with George on Christmas Day, Johnathon?" Somehow, I did not want to hear his answer.

Johnathon looked through his tears and sadly shook his little head. "Techr, I didn't have a chance to play with ole George. When I went out to find him, I didn't see ole George nowhere. So I called him. I said, 'George!

George! Come to Johnathon, George!' But,Techr, ole George wuz across the road, and when he heard me callin' him, he lit off, runnin' as fast as he could to git to me, but, Techr! A car wuz comin' down the road real fast, and it hit my George and knocked him over in the street. I runned out in the street to git him, Techr! But when I got to him, his li'l body wuz still, and his li'l feet didn't move, and his li'l stubby tail didn't wag no more, Techr, and his eyes, they jest looked straight and didn't look at me. Techr! I grabbed up my George and runned in the house to ask my Mommy to take him to the dog doctor, but Mommy said it wuz good riddance that George had got hit by the car. She said that she couldn't 'ford to feed that ole fleabag no way."

Johnathon dropped his little, head and his body was racked with sobs. I reached over and put my arms around him, trying in some small way to console this tortured child of six. "Oh, Johnathon! I'm so sorry!"

After a few moments, Johnathon looked up at me, his little voice quivering and his eyes swollen from crying. "I don't know what riddance means, Techr, but it can't be good 'cause my George got dead that day on Christmas, and that's why I don't like Christmas, Techr. On Christmas Day I lost the only thing in the world what loved me, my George, and now I don't have nobody to love me, Techr!" Johnathon started crying loudly again, digging into his swollen eyes with tightly, clinched fists. And suddenly, I remembered!

"Johnathon! I forgot to tell you! There's a present here for you! I ran to my closet and pulled out a little rectangular box that was wrapped in brightly, colored green and red Christmas paper. It had a big, red bow on the top. I walked back to Johnathon and handed it to him. "Here, Johnathon! It's for you. Open it!"

"For me, Techr! Are ya' sure? Does it say Johnathon?"

"Yes it does! Look at the label, Johnathon! Look at the letters!"

Johnathon reluctantly took the package from my hands and started spelling out the letters. "J..O..H..N..A…Techr!! It DOES say Johnathon! J..O..H..N..A..T..H..O..N…. J..O..H..N..A..T..H..O..N.. Techr! It's my name! Johnathon! But, Techr! How did it git here? Where did it come from?"

I shrugged my shoulders and tried to look as puzzled as Johnathon did.

"Techr, do ya' s'pose Santa Claus left it here for me 'cause he didn't know where I wuz? I bet that's it, Techr! I moved so much he couldn't find me! Ya' think so, Techr?"

"Could be, Johnathon. Why don't you open it and see what's inside?"

"Okay, Techr." Johnathon tore into the present, slinging ribbons and paper with a flourish. His eyes widened as he discovered a little doctor's kit inside the wrappings. "Techr! It's a doctor's kit! Oh, Techr! It's a doctor's kit! Ain't this jest the best doctor's kit that ya' ever did see?" Johnathon picked up the little box and hugged it to his heart. Suddenly, he looked back at me with wide eyes. "Techr! Ya' think I better write to Santa Claus and thank him for this doctor's kit?"

I smiled at the dear child. "I think that would be a very good idea, Johnathon."

Johnathon looked back at me with pleading eyes. "Will ya' help me, Techr? I might not 'member how to spell all the words."

"Sure, Johnathon. I'll be happy to help you write your letter."

Johnathon slid over in his little desk. "You can sit beside me, Techr." I sat beside Johnathon and put one arm around his little shoulders. He leaned into me, briefly, and laid his head against my shoulder. "Thank ya', Techr. You so nice, Techr! I love you!"

Johnathon and I wrote a grand letter to Santa Claus that day. Well, actually, Johnathon wrote 'DEAR,' and I wrote the rest, because every word he wanted to tell Santa, he couldn't 'member' how to spell. When the letter was finished, Johnathon picked it up and looked at it proudly.

"Doncha' think this is a good letter, Techr? I do! Oh, Techr! Ya' write so purty!" Johnathon suddenly started comparing the writing in the letter with the writing from the wrapping paper. His little head looked up and down from the note to the writing on the Christmas tag. "Ya' know som'em,' Techr? I believe ya' write jest like Santa Claus!"

TWELVE

YES, I GAVE JOHNATHON the little doctor's kit that day. I told him it would be our little secret, and you know…I don't believe that he ever told a soul about it. But I saw a change in Johnathon from that day on, and he literally became my shadow.

He stood outside the classroom each morning and waited for me to come down the hall. Then his face would break into a huge smile, and he would reach up and carry my books and other things into the classroom. He would then tidy my desk and run to hang my coat in the closet. He followed me to the sink in the room every time I went there to wash my hands, and he would stand, patiently waiting, holding a paper towel for me to dry my hands. Johnathon was always glued to me at lunch and somehow managed to place himself in just the right spot so that he would end up at my table.

Rather than sit with the other teachers at recess, I usually played with the children in my class. After Christmas,

Johnathon and I played ball with the boys, jumped rope with the girls, and joined in the chases when the current "sweethearts" needed to tell each other " first grade love secrets." Even when I tried to get Johnathon to go and play with the other children without me, he refused, politely, of course.

"If you are going to play, Techr, I'll play. But if you ain't, then I'll stay with you. You jest might need me to do something for ya." I really heard that answer a lot, and pretty soon, everyone in the school knew that wherever they saw me, Johnathon would not be far behind.

The funny thing is that I thrived on Johnathon's affection for me, and he thrived because he knew that I loved him. I loved all of the other children in my class, too, but Johnathon was special. He was the closest thing that I had ever had to a child of my own, I guess.

The days clicked by at an alarming rate that winter. The students became expert first grade readers, and by Valentine's Day, their writing skills were so perfected that I suggested they make all of their valentines, instead of buying them. Well, I used the excuse about their writing to keep the bought cards out of the classroom. Actually, I knew that Johnathon would not be able to buy any valentines, and I wanted his to be just like the rest.

So for the first two weeks in February, the children and I stopped our classwork an hour before time to go home and made valentines. Shortly before Valentine's Day, I encouraged the children to make one giant, special valentine for someone very dear to them. I told them it could be a parent, grandparent, or a special friend. I provided lace, ribbons, glitter, and colored paints for them to use on this very, important card.

The children went to work with a fervor, excitedly whispering to each other about the special cards and who would receive them. I watched Johnathon as he worked on this last, precious card and knew in my heart that I would end up with his. Oh, life was so sweet!

Valentine's Day dawned with gray skies and a classroom full of chattering children, taking their turns in putting their homemade cards in the decorated boxes on each person's desk. Johnathon patiently awaited his turn, often looking at me as if he had a big secret that he just could not wait to tell. I smiled at him throughout the morning, knowing that a giant card would soon be placed in my box when his turn came around.

"It's your turn, Johnathon!" called Kathy as she delivered her last Valentine to her best friend's box.

Johnathon got up slowly from his desk and gathered up his assortment of homemade valentines. He slowly walked around the room, placing each one in the gaily, colored boxes. Finally, he was down to the last two valentines, one small one, and the huge, special one that was adorned with ribbons and hearts and child-drawn flowers. Johnathon looked at me shyly. He then walked up to my desk and dropped in the small, roughly-made card. With a shrug of his shoulders and a somewhat hopeful look, he turned and walked back to the newest student in the room, a little girl named Tara, who had long, brown hair; big, nearly-black eyes; and the sweetest smile this side of Heaven. Johnathon shyly placed his special card in Tara's colored box, hunched his head down into his shoulders, dug his hands into his old, jeans' pockets, and crept back to his desk.

Immediately, a chorus of voices began. "Johnathon loves Tara! Johnathon loves Tara! Johnathon and Tara's sweethearts!"

I should have stopped the children from their taunts, but I just sat there, watching to see what would happen. Amazingly enough, Johnathon didn't get angry at all. He just sat in his desk, all hunkered down, peering at me with those huge eyes of his. I was totally baffled. First, because a little six-year-old girl with long, brown hair had gotten my valentine, and secondly, that Johnathon was oblivious to the teasing of the rest of the children.

Amid the commotion in the classroom, Tara got up from her seat to deliver her valentines. When she passed Johnathon's desk, she put a small valentine in his box. As she started to go on to the next desk, she suddenly turned and said, quietly, "Thank you, Johnathon. I like your valentine best of all."

Johnathon looked up at me with the smile of the century on his face. His circle of people who cared about him had just doubled. "Techr" loved him, and the little girl named Tara did, too. The irony of it all was that I was jealous! I was pea-green jealous of a six-year-old girl who loved my little Johnathon!

THIRTEEN

WHEN I FINALLY ADJUSTED to the fact that Johnathon had two "girls" in his life, things settled down to normal in my classroom. Sweet, little Tara gradually took my place in Johnathon's obsessive adoration, and he started to follow her around instead of me. But that was okay. I knew that Johnathon desperately needed friends his own age, and that kind, little girl with the long, brown hair fit the bill perfectly. Actually, I finally had more time to give to the rest of the class when Johnathon's affections focused on Tara.

One week after Valentine's Day, I awoke to a white, blanket of snow that transformed my small town to a winter wonderland. School was called off for the day, so I used the time to catch up on grading some papers and cleaning house. The snow continued to fall throughout the day, and by nightfall, five inches had accumulated, with more threatening to fall during the night.

With my husband out of town at a convention, I felt an uneasiness as I settled on the sofa to watch the evening news. I sipped on a hot cup of Russian Tea as I listened to the local commentator talk about the weather conditions. The last thing I remember him saying was to stay off of the roads if at all possible. I guess the quietness of the steadily falling snow and the monotone of the television lulled me to sleep as I snuggled into the cozy afghans that Mom had generously placed in each room of my house.

The shrill ringing of the telephone startled me from my deep slumber, and I fumbled over my head to reach the annoying intruder of my dreams.

"Hello," I mumbled into the phone with my eyes still closed, hoping the call would be brief so that I could go back to my land of dreams.

"Elly? This is Barbara Rice."

"Who?" I didn't recognize the voice on the other end of the line.

"Barbara Rice. Your principal. You do remember me, don't you? You know, you've only been out of school for one snow day, Elly. Don't forget me so fast."

"Oh, Mrs. Rice! I'm sorry! I didn't recognize your voice, and I must confess that I was napping on the couch when you called. I guess we'll be out again tomorrow, right?"

"Yes, Elly. It looks like the snow is setting in for the rest of the week. But that's not why I called. Have you been watching the news?"

I thought back to when I first dozed off. "Uh, yes, I did watch the weather report before I dropped off to sleep. Why?"

"Elly, I'm afraid something terrible has happened. A man by the name of Brent Adams was released from prison today, and when he walked in his house, he found his wife in the bed with another man. He killed him, Elly. Brent Adams killed the man he found with his wife. It's all over the news right now."

"Do I know this Brent Adams, Mrs. Rice? And who did he kill?"

"Elly, Brent Adams is Johnathon's father! The man he killed is Jack Greene. Elly, Jack Greene is the same man who left Johnathon at school that day and told him to find another place to live. Remember?"

I dropped the phone and put my hands over my mouth. This just couldn't be true! Not to my Johnathon! He was just starting to get his little life together. Why? How could this happen now?

I left the phone dangling beside the couch and stood up. I forgot that Mrs. Rice was still on the line. I forgot to hang up the phone. I almost forgot to breathe. All I could think about was my poor, little Johnathon and what he must be going through. I had to get to him. He needed me. I had to find him.

I hastily threw on some jeans and a bulky sweater. Grabbing a jacket from the hall closet, I opened the door and ran down the snow-laden steps, throwing caution to the wind as I trudged through the snowdrifts to my car. I used my bare hands to wipe away the snow from the windshield, and somehow, I didn't feel the cold at all. For my mind was numb to pain or cold. All I could think about was Johnathon.

The engine of my little car started immediately as if it knew that I needed it to be my loyal friend in this mission of mercy. I backed out of the driveway and slowly made my way through the treacherous roads to Commerce Street. Circular lights from the police cars were flashing through the swirling snow as I neared the scene, and bright, yellow crime tape already surrounded the little house that Johnathon called home. I pulled over to the curb and jumped out of my car. A policeman stopped me as I tried to come near the house.

"Sorry, Lady. You can't go in there. This ain't no party, you know."

"I need to find, Johnathon. I'm his teacher, and I need to find him!"

"I don't know a Johnathon, Ma'am. Does he live here?"

"Yes, he's a little boy. He's Brent Adams' little boy. Where is he? I have to find him. I know he needs me!"

"Oh, both boys, Ma'am, were taken to a neighbor's house down the street. They sure went through a lot here tonight. I understand they both saw what their old man did to that fella."

My heart sank when I heard that. I didn't know how much more Johnathon could take. "Sir, can you direct me to the house where the boys were taken?"

"I don't rightly know, Ma'am. All I know it was a neighbor lady who took the boys for the night while their mother is down at headquarters."

I thought for a minute. Miss Ada! I just knew that it had to be Miss Ada who had come to the rescue of Johnathon and Willie.

I ran down the street, slipping in the snow as I went. I searched my brain to remember the place where Miss Ada lived. I guess that it must be true that God looks after fools and children, because somehow, I ended up on Miss Ada's porch in no time. I bammed on the door with my fist. After a few moments, the charitable, lady known to the community as Miss Ada opened the door.

"Why, ain't you that nice teacher from Johnathon's school?"

"Yes, Ma'am, Miss Ada, I'm Elly Harris. Do you have Johnathon and Willie? I just have to see Johnathon and let him know that I'm here for him. Tell me he's here, Miss Ada!"

"Yes, he's here. Little Willie went on to sleep, but only the good Lord knows how that little tyke was able to after the mess they jest seen. It was jest plain awful, Miz Harris; jest awful, I tell you."

"Where is Johnathon, Miss Ada? Is he okay?"

"Well, Johnathon's another story, Miz Harris. He's jest sitting on the floor in that room yonder. He won't move and jest sits there and stares. Meybe you can get him to answer ya', Miz Harris. Heaven knows I've tried, but he don't seem to hear me."

I walked into the bedroom and had to focus my eyes in the dark before I spotted Johnathon crouched in the corner of the room. I walked over and knelt down beside him. He didn't move or look up at me.

I put my hand on his leg. "Johnathon? It's me, Techr. Can you hear me? I came to see if you needed me, Johnathon. I wanted to make sure that you were all right."

Johnathon's weary, tormented eyes slowly focused on me, and a huge tear rolled down his face. He just stared at me for what seemed like an eternity and finally reached over and put his dirty, little hand on my face. He started to speak, but only one word came out very quietly. "Techr."

I grabbed Johnathon and hugged him to me. He hugged me back with a fierceness that nearly took my breath away. Great, gulping sobs racked his little body as we sat in the floor of Miss Ada's house in the dark. When his heart-rending crying subsided to sniffles, I reached down and took his face in my hands.

"I'm here, Johnathon. Don't worry. Techr's here."

We stayed on the floor for a long time, just Johnathon and me, arm in arm, until his little head dropped over in an exhausted sleep. After a while, I gently lifted him and put him on the bed next to little Willie.

By the time I reached my home, it was early in the morning. The snow was still falling as I lay across my bed and fell into a troubled sleep. It was nearly noon when I finally awoke.

A quick phone call to Miss Ada's gave me the news I had expected. Johnathon and Willie had been taken by the Department of Social Services early that morning to be placed in a foster home until the boys' mother was able to take care of them.

Once again Johnathon's world was turned upside-down. Once again he had to adjust to a new place and new people and new rules. Once again Johnathon's security was shattered, this time with a permament break down of the family as he knew it. Murder One would probably remove Brent Adams from Johnathon's life forever, and I couldn't decide if I was sad or glad because of Johnathon's loss. I do know I was elated that Johnathon would not have to dodge any more whiskey bottles!

FOURTEEN

IT'S FUNNY how during my year with Johnathon, the things that usually excited me, like snow and days off from school, moved way down my priority list. I was actually glad when the sun finally popped out over my Carolina home on Sunday morning, and the snow started to melt.

All afternoon I watched the clock tick slowly on the mantle, and all I could think about was Johnathon. I knew that he was physically all right, tucked away probably in a surrounding town in a foster home. I hoped and prayed that his temporary parents would find the time to listen to him and to comfort him during the time he was there. I figured it would be several weeks before I would see him again.

Monday morning dawned crisp and clear, with only a few errant patches of snow remaining in the ditches and shady areas around town. I eagerly rushed off to school in hopes of hearing some news about Johnathon.

No one seemed to know any more details about Johnathon or the situation with the murder, so I headed down to my classroom. With my eyes averted to the floor tiles, I answered the greetings of the children as if I was a robot, until I reached the door of my classroom. Suddenly, I heard the sweetest voice that God ever created.

"Mornin' Techr! Want me to take ya' things in the room for ya?"

I jerked my head up and looked into those beautiful, brown eyes that had haunted me for five days. "Johnathon! Whatever are you doing here?" I dropped everything that I was carrying in the floor and knelt down and hugged Johnathon to me.

"I come on the bus like I always do, Techr." Johnathon pulled away from me and put his grimy, little hand on my face. "Why ya' crying, Techr? You sad 'cause the snow melted?"

As I looked at this dear child, who had just witnessed his father kill another man, the tears would not stop. In spite of everything, Johnathon still thought like a child, but had the wisdom of Solomon.

"No, Johnathon, I'm really glad the snow is gone. I wanted to come back to school. And I'm not sad, Johnathon. I'm just glad to see you. I didn't think you'd be here today. Where did you stay last night?"

"My Mommy come and got me and Willie from cross town where I stayed last time. Mommy said it's jest us now, me and her and li'l Willie. She said not to 'spect for Daddy to come back 'cause o' what he did to Jack." Johnathon dropped his head and kicked at the floor with his old shoes, and his mood changed from excitement to melancholic in a matter of moments.

Using all of the teacher skills that I could remember, I straightened up and grabbed Johnathon's hand. "Well, I am so glad that you are here today, Johnathon! I am going to need you to help me get the room back in order before the other students arrive. Will you help me?"

Johnathon looked up at me, and a gigantic smile lit up his little face. "Oh, yes, ma'am, Techr! I'll help ya! I'll be ya' helper all day if ya' want me to!"

Johnathon hurriedly picked up my books and scurried into the room. He neatly placed my things on my desk, re-arranged the desk a bit, blew dust off with his mouth, and skipped to the back of the room to start putting down the students' desks. I heard him humming "Jesus Loves Me" as he worked to get the room in order

My solid, southern, religious faith was put to a tremendous test that day as I watched Johnathon, busying about the room, humming that old, familiar chorus. I guess I can really thank Johnathon for helping me to get back on track; for as I watched him, it dawned on me that Johnathon, himself, in spite of the fact that he was abused, neglected, a witness to murder, and in a house with no Santa Claus or Christmas Tree, still held on to his faith, even when it seemed that 'God didn't have time to listen to him.'

Later that day, Johnathon's faith and endurance were put to another test, and I'm afraid, this time, his patience just wore out. Right after lunch, the children and I went outside for recess. We hadn't been out long when I noticed that a bunch of the boys, headed by Patrick Martin, made their way over to where Johnathon and Tara were swinging. Before I could react in any way, arms and legs were flying everywhere in a cloud of dust!

I ran across the playground as fast as I could. Several of the girls were running to get me as I approached the scene. "Miz Harris! Miz Harris! Johnathon's beating Patrick Martin up!"

Well, sure enough, there on the ground lay Patrick, bruised and bleeding, with Johnathon sitting astride him, punching him with his fists. I quickly pulled Johnathon off of Patrick and yelled for him to stand back while I checked Patrick's wounds. Patrick jumped up and started to cry.

"He hit me, Miz Harris! That dirty, mean, Johnathon, with a jailbird Daddy, hit me, and I'm going to tell my Daddy, and he'll be sorry!"

I looked back at Johnathon who was red in the face and breathing heavily. "Why did you hit Patrick, Johnathon?"

"Cause he called me names, Techr. He said I wuz a jailbird jest like my Daddy, and that his Daddy said he didn't want me in the same class as Patrick, and that he wuz goin' to see to it that I got moved to another class so Patrick didn't have to stay in the same class with a jailbird's son!" Johnathon was gasping for breath as he finished his story. I looked around at the other children who had gathered near the boys.

"Johnathon's right, Miz Harris! I heard Patrick say those things. He shoved Johnathon, too! I saw him!"

Todd stood very close to Johnathon as he verified what had happened.

"I saw him, too, Miz Harris! He just came right up to where me and Johnathon were swinging and started saying those awful things to Johnathon. He shoved Johnathon first. Then, Johnathon hit him!" Tara cut her eye around to see if Johnathon was listening to her stand up for him.

"I didn't do nothing to him! I just walked by, minding my own business, and Johnathon jumped me! He just started beating on me for no reason, and I'm going to tell my Daddy!"

Patrick stuck to his story even when his Daddy came to the school to get him. Of course, Patrick's father believed everything his boy said, and true to his word, he petitioned Mrs. Rice to place Johnathon in another class. To quote Mr. Martin, our distinquished board member, he said, "I don't want my son to be in the same class with riffraff trash!"

Mrs. Rice did honor Mr. Martin's request to have the two boys in separate classes. But she didn't move Johnathon. The next day, when I arrived at school, I had a note in my box from my principal. It said:

"Mrs. Harris, I believe it is in the best interest of all involved if Johnathon Adams and Patrick Martin be separated for the remainder of the school year. Therefore I am placing Patrick in Mrs. Coleman's first grade class, and Johnathon will remain with you. I hope that will be satisfactory with you. Barbara Rice"

When I looked up from the note I had been reading as I walked to my room that morning, I smiled. I said a quick prayer that I had an understanding principal who stood up for what was right. Mrs. Rice knew that Johnathon needed me. What she didn't realize was that I needed Johnathon just as much!

With a spring in my step, I headed down the hall. If I had strained my eyes a bit, I would have seen the ragtag boy in the dirty, Braves tee shirt, standing outside my classroom, jumping up and down and waving to me. If I had strained my ears a little, I would have heard the familiar, childish voice, calling, "Techr! Techr! Can I help ya' today!"

FIFTEEN

WHEN I TRY TO PUT TOGETHER the rest of February of that year, it's kind of a blur. I do know that no one ever picked on Johnathon again about his father being in jail. Actually, Johnathon benefited a bit from the situation. For some reason, maybe the fact that he put Patrick Martin in his place, Johnathon became the class hero. The boys vied for Johnathon's attention at recess, and the girls all decided to be "sweethearts" with him. Of course, Johnathon remained true to his first "love" and continued to be best friends with little Tara.

So February eased into March, and I watched with pride as my little first grade class embraced Johnathon as their unsung hero, leader, and friend. It, indeed, was like a breath of fresh air to know that Johnathon was, at last, beating the odds and coming out on top.

I should have known that victory does often have its sting. For no sooner did Johnathon start feeling good about himself, than the bottom fell out of his world again, and I was not able to foresee or protect him from the hurt he endured this time.

On a particularly windy day in early March, Johnathon didn't come to school. It was the first day he had missed in a long time, and I became uneasy as the day wore on. I remembered that Johnathon had appeared to be fine the day before and had even promised to bring me a picture of him and Willie that had been taken by Miss Ada's son during the snow.

When school let out that day, I grabbed my things and headed, once again, for Commerce Street to check on Johnathon. After knocking on the door, repeatedly, and getting no response, I walked down the street to where Miss Ada lived. She was sitting on her porch, rocking in an old, decrepit rocker.

"I figured you'd be a'comin' around this evenin,' Miz Harris. Guess you already heard 'bout the boys." Miss Ada kept a steady beat with the rocking chair as she spoke to me.

"No, Miss Ada, I haven't heard. Where is Johnathon?"

Miss Ada reached into her soiled, apron pocket and took out a dingy hankerchief. She blew her nose, loudly, as she continued. "I shore hate to be the one to tell you this, Miz Harris, but both o'those boys is in the hospital. They both beat up pretty bad, I tell you!"

I sank to the steps, but my heart sank further. "What! What happened?"

"All I knows, Miz Harris, is that 'bout twelve o'clock last night, there was a loud commotion over at the Adams' place, screaming and yelling and all, and I called the law. I didn't know but what that ole sorry daddy of Johnathon's and little Willlie's had busted outta jail or something, so I called the law. Well, it wudden long 'fore the police got there, and I wuz watchin' from my porch here. They wudden in there long when an ambulance came screeching up, and both those little boys wuz loaded on the ambulance and took to County General. Then, the police took their Mama, in handcuffs, mind you, and rode off with her to jail, I guess."

"What did she do to Johnathon and Willie?" I screamed.

"Well, Miz Harris, I sent my boy down to the hospital to see 'bout those boys, and it 'peared that their mama done beat them to a pulp! I don't rightly know what she wuz so mad about, but she done put little Willie in the 'tensive care with her craziness, and my boy says that Johnathon got hisself a broke arm. He'll be all right, but I don't know 'bout Willie now. I jest don't know." Miss Ada continued to rock back and forth as she stared off into space.

A feeling of urgency crept over me. I had to get to the hospital to see about Johnathon and little Willie. I stumbled over my own feet as I literally ran to my car. As I raced off in the direction of the hospital, I suddenly remembered that I had not even thanked Miss Ada for the information. But I'm not sure that she would have heard me. She was mourning those two little boys, too.

Luckily, I did not get caught for speeding as I broke all records, getting across town to the hospital. I quickly found a place to park and ran into the building. After checking at the front desk, I headed for the pediatrics floor. I stopped for a brief moment outside room 401 and tried to calm myself. Johnathon needed 'Techr' to be mature and steady, not out of control like the other adults in his life.

I slowly walked into his room, and there on the sterile hospital bed lay my little Johnathon. He had a tube for fluids in his right arm, and the other arm was in a cast of bright, white plaster. A small bandage covered his left eyebrow, and his top lip was swollen out of shape. His eyes were closed, and I thought he must be asleep.

I stood near the bed and just looked at this dear child while hot, angry tears gushed from my eyes. I squeezed my eyes shut to block out the ugly thoughts that were racing through my mind when I heard a weak voice.

"Techr! Why ya' crying, Techr? I'm all right. Don't cry, Techr! My arm don't hurt much."

I looked through my tears to that same, forgiving, little face, so full of expectations, that I had come to love over the past year. "Johnathon! Are you okay?"

"Oh, yes, ma'am, Techr. I'm okay. The doctor says I'll be right as rain in a few weeks. And I can still use my other hand to write in school, Techr, so ya' don't have to worry." A frown creased Johnathon's brow as he looked at me. "Techr, is li'l Willie all right? He went to sleep on the ride over here last night. He's okay, ain't he, Techr?"

"Yes, Johnathon," I lied. "Willie's okay. He's in another room and is still sleeping." I just couldn't tell Johnathon that Willie was in a coma with head injuries. I just didn't feel like he could handle anymore bad news. "Johnathon, can you tell me what happened last night?"

Johnathon dropped his head and became very tense and serious. Finally, after several minutes, he looked back at me with those enormous eyes peering out from under his eyebrows. "I didn't mean to make Mommy mad, Techr! She wuz already mad at li'l Willie for spillin' his cereal, and she wuz feelin' so bad that she had to take some o' my Daddy's medcine from his bottle that he left under the bed. So, I shouldna' asked her 'bout Jack."

With a puzzled look on my face, I looked at this poor, tormented child. "What about, Jack, Johnathon? What did you ask?"

"I jest asked Mommy if she reckoned Jack wuz in Heaven since my Daddy killed him and all. But I shouldna' asked 'bout Jack 'cause Mommy don't like to talk 'bout him no more. So she slapped me in the mouth and told me to shut up talkin' 'bout Jack. But I jest went on, Techr, like I didn't hear her or something. I wuz bad to do that, Techr. I said that I bet Jack didn't go to Heaven 'cause he wuz so mean, and that's when my Mommy hit me up side my head, and it knocked me over into Willie's highchair, and he fell over in the spilled cereal. He started yelling real loud, Techr, and my Mommy hit him over and over in the face so he would stop crying. And, Techr, I run out on the porch and started screaming, and it wudden long 'fore the poleece come and the ambliunce, too, and the men in it put a big, ole, white thang on my arm and my head, and they took little Willie and put all kinds o' things on him and drove real fast to bring us here. But they didn't let my Mommy come, Techr. Wonder why they didn't let Mommy come, Techr? She ain't come yet. Ya' reckon she's still mad at us, Techr?"

I looked at this battered, abused child and marveled that he could still care for a mother who had just beat him and his little brother nearly to death. "Don't worry about your Mommy, Johnathon. You just get some rest so you will feel better. We all miss you at school and want you back real soon."

"Okay, Techr, I'll rest and get all better real quick. Tell everybody I said hey and don't forgit to tell Tara. She's my best friend, ya' know." Johnathon's eyes started to get heavy, and in a few minutes he appeared to be asleep.

I held his hand, careful to avoid the tube running from it, until it went limp in my hands. Laying it down easily on the bed, I leaned over to kiss Johnathon on the forehead. His eyes opened briefly. "I love ya, Techr."

The tears in my eyes started again as I watched this precious child give in to sleep. I couldn't tell him about Willie, and I certainly couldn't tell him that his mother had been taken to jail for child abuse the night before. Now both of Johnathon's parents were incarcerated, little Willie was fighting for his life, and six-year-old Johnathon was virtually all alone to face life.

I walked down the corridor of the hospital, absorbed in misery and pity, and made my way to the chapel at the end of the hall. I fled to the front pew, knelt down and begged God to spare little Willie. About ten o'clock that night, I finally went home. But I didn't stay very long. After telling my dear, patient husband the story about the boys, he looked at me and smiled. He knew, as well as I did, what I had to do.

I grabbed some clean clothes, a toothbursh, and my bookbag, and headed back to the hospital. Children need a parent to stay by their sides when they are in the hospital, and I was the nearest thing Johnathon and Willie had to a parent right then.

I didn't miss school the next day. I was a little wrinkled, and I probably needed a bath in the worst kind of way, but I was there for my other students when the eight o'clock bell rang to start the day.

I don't know if Johnathon even knew that I stayed with him that night. But that was all right. I was there if he needed me, and that was all that mattered.

SIXTEEN

I GUESS THE LORD was listening to a distraught, troubled teacher that year, because Willie did come out of the coma the next day, and he and Johnathon were released a few days later to the Department of Social Services. The boys didn't go to a foster home this time. They were immediately placed in a home for abused children that was provided for the county through charitable organizations.

On Monday morning Johnathon was brought to school by a nice, old gentleman by the name of Mr. "Bill," who worked as a volunteer in the home. He told me that he would be bringing Johnathon back and forth to school as long as Johnathon remained in the home.

After "Mr. Bill" left, I looked at the little fellow standing beside me in the doorway. His lip was healing, although it had a nasty, jagged scab running across it. A big bruise over his eye was starting to turn yellow, and his left arm was resting, neatly, in a pristine, white, arm sling.

"I'm sorry I wuzn't here to carry ya' things in the room this mornin', Techr. But I'll try to get "Mr. Bill" to bring me earlier in the mornin' so I can help ya."

Just as a new flood of tears started to build in my eyes, the other children saw Johnathon and came running to the door.

"Johnathon! Johnathon! What happened to your arm?"

"Johnathon! What happened to your mouth?"

"Johanthon! You been in a wreck?"

Johnathon cut his eyes up at me, and I knew I had to come to his rescue, again. "Boys and girls! Johnathon had an accident, but he's going to be just fine now. I want you all to help him until his arm gets better."

"I'll carry your lunch tray, Johnathon!" Todd quickly said.

"I'll carry your books for you, Johnathon!"

"I'll help you with your work!"

A chorus of voices offered Johnathon more help than he really needed, but the love and support of the other children for their wounded friend was probably the best medicine Johnathon could have received that day. It did my heart good to stand on the sidelines and let the rest of the class take care of Johnathon for a change.

During the next few weeks Johnathon came to school clean, rested and always with his homework in his hand. Each day his cast sported more names in bright colors, and I really believe that he was a little sorry when the cast was removed.

Johnathon's mother was kept in jail during those bright, spring days when Johanthon was thriving at school. She could not post bail, so she had to stay put until her trial came up in June. I know that I should have felt pity for her, but I didn't. I was glad that she was out of Johnathon's and Willie's lives for a while. I really hoped that that they would never have to live with her again.

Johnathon did mention his mother to me on occasion, but, for the most part, his days were happy and carefree while he was staying in the home for abused children.

On the eleventh of April, Johnathon came to school as he always did. He went to his desk and started his morning math while I checked the roll and carried out the routine for the morning. When we started to fill in the date for the calendar, I asked the class if anyone had a birthday that day. When no one answered, I looked at Johnathon.

"Johnathon? Isn't your birthday today?"

Johnathon glanced up from his work and shrugged his shoulders. "Yes, Ma'am, Techr. Today's my birthday if it's April eleventh." He looked back down at his work and continued to write.

I wrote Johnathon's name on the calendar and walked back to his desk to carry him the birthday crown to wear for the day. He looked at me with a puzzled look and, reluctantly, put the crown on his head. When the class joined me in singing "Happy Birthday" to Johnathon, he looked at us strangely, then continued on with his work. I leaned over and whispered in Johnathon's ear.

"Don't you like birthdays, Johnathon?"

"Well, I guess so, Techr, since I'm seven today. And, Techr, I ain't never had nobody sing to me 'fore. That wuz kinda nice, too." Johnathon went back to his work and didn't mention his birthday all morning. He even left the birthday crown on his desk when we went to lunch.

When Johnathon sat down beside me with his tray of food, I couldn't stand it any longer. "Johnathon, have you ever had a birthday party?"

Johnathon looked up from his food with a frown across his brow. "No, Ma'am, Techr. My Mommy said birthdays jest cause you to get old and ugly, and they ain't nothin' special."

I knew I should have left it alone, but I just couldn't. "Well, Johnathon, have you ever been given a present on your birthday?"

Johnathon shook his head and looked down in his plate. "Well, I don't know if this counts, Techr, but Miss Ada, she gives me some presents from her boy sometimes, ya' know, clothes and stuff, but I don't think she ever give 'em to me on my birthday."

"Johnathon, have you ever had a birthday cake?" I knew what the answer would be before Johnathon opened his mouth.

"No, Techr. I ain't never had no birthday cake. But Mommy made Daddy one for his birthday once, and he threw it in the floor and said it wudden fittin' to eat, so Mommy said she wudden never make no more and she didn't neither." Johnathon dropped his head and continued to eat his lunch. For some reason, I lost my appetite that day.

I had another teacher watch my class at recess while I made a quick phone call to the local bakery. They promised me a brightly, decorated birthday cake by two o'clock that afternoon.

Promptly at two, there was a knock on our classroom door. I opened the door, and there stood Mrs. Rice holding a delicious-looking, chocolate cake with "Happy Birthday, Johnathon" written on the top in big, yellow icing.

"I have a delivery for Johnathon Adams," Mrs. Rice announced, proudly.

Johnathon looked up and just sat there as in a stupor. Finally, at the urging of the other children, Johnathon walked over to the door and stared at the cake. "Is this for me, Miz Rice? Ya' got the right Johnathon?"

"Yes, sir. You're the birthday boy today, aren't you?" Mrs. Rice smiled at Johnathon as she put the cake on the table in the front of the room.

Johnathon looked up at me, and I just shrugged my shoulders. "I don't know, Johnathon. I guess someone remembered it was your birthday today."

Johnathon's face broke into a huge grin as he looked from the beautiful cake to me. He motioned with his finger for me to lean down so he could tell me a secret. "I know where the cake come from, Techr. My Mommy. She 'membered."

SEVENTEEN

I SERIOUSLY DOUBT that Johnathon's mother gave a thought to her oldest son when his birthday rolled around. She remained incarcerated in the local jail, awaiting trial for her abuse to her two children. Her only contact with the outside world, that I know about, was through the attorney the court appointed to represent her. I kept up with her case through a lawyer friend of mine, and fervently hoped that the judicial system would throw the book at her for her abusive and neglectful treatment of Johnathon and little Willie.

In the meantime, Johnathon thrived! With his arm neatly mended and a safe and secure environment in which to live, he made great strides in his schoolwork. He came to school in clean, pressed clothes, and even his face took on a healthy, rosy glow that indicated he was eating properly for a change. I can't help but believe that his happiness during that time contributed to his general well-being.

I guess it was a lucky thing for Johnathon that the yearly achievement and IQ tests were given during the time he was living in the home for abused children. I shudder to think how he would have performed if he had been home with his mother. As it turned out, Johnathon scored the highest of all of the first graders on the achievement section of the test for our school that year. Mrs. Rice seemed surprised when the results came back, but I didn't. I had already figured out that I had been dead wrong with my early judgments of Johnathon's capabilities. The fact that Johnathon had one of the highest IQ's in the school did cause me to wonder a bit. It just didn't seem possible for those sorry, ignorant parents of his to be able to produce such a bright child.

About the middle of April, I started working on our class play that I always presented in the spring of the year. After looking over my wiggly, little first graders, I decided the play, "Peter Rabbit," fit my students perfectly.

There weren't many speaking parts, except for Flopsey, Mopsey, Cottontail, and, of course, Peter. The other parts consisted of a cadre of various animals and supporting rolls for the main characters. I had the children take home the script over a week-end and learn a few lines so that I could decide who would get the main parts.

When Monday morning arrived, I rounded the corner and went down the hall, as usual, to my classroom, only to find Johnathon waiting frantically for me.

"Techr! Techr! I know my lines! I know 'em by heart! Wanna hear me say 'em?" Johnathon jumped up and down, very much like a bunny in the upcoming play.

"Johnathon! I'm so glad you learned your lines. Can you wait to tell them to me when the rest of the class gets here?"

Johnathon looked up at me with those bright, beautiful eyes of his. "I dunno, Techr. I'll try my best to wait, but I might jest have to bust open and tell ya' my lines if I can't wait! They jest keep wantin' to come right outta my mouth!"

Trying to control my laughter, I put my finger on Johnathon's upper lip. "Well, try real hard to keep them in your mouth, Johnathon, until everyone is here so I can hear all the children try out for the parts, okay?"

Johnathon looked up and answered through his tight lips. "I'll try, Techr."

Well, I didn't get to even call the roll that morning or take the lunch count, because every few seconds I heard, "I'm bustin,' Techr. I'm 'bout to bust! Hurry, Techr! My mouth's 'bustin!"

Hoping the attendance clerk and the lunchroom manager would forgive me for being late with my reports, I stopped and looked at the class. "I believe that we will go ahead with the try-outs for the play, since some of you are so excited about saying your lines for me. Johnathon, I wonder if you would like to go first."

Johnathon didn't have to get up from his seat. He was already half-way to the front of the room, jumping up and down in his excitement. He immediately crouched down in a bunny stance, wiggled his nose, and started hopping across the floor to get into 'Mr. McGregor's' garden. The class roared with laughter as Johnathon pretended to steal cabbages and carrots from the imaginary garden. He recited his lines as he acted out the part of the bunny thief, and I couldn't help but think that maybe he had some prior experience in the act of stealing, because he was such a pro at it.

When Johnathon finished his rendition of Peter, the whole class begged me to let Johnathon be Peter in the play. I acted like I was giving it some serious thought as I looked at Johnathon with my finger lightly tapping my forehead.

"Well, I guess Johnathon would make a good Peter Rabbit. Would you like the part, Johnathon?"

Johnathon's brown eyes got about as big as saucers. "Oh, yes, Ma'am, Techr! I sure do wanna be Peter Rabbit. And I'll be the best Peter Rabbit ya' ever did see, too!"

So for the next three weeks, the class and I worked every spare minute on our production of "Peter Rabbit." One of the mothers made bunny costumes, and Linda McCord, the art teacher, made us an elaborate set for the stage.

All of the children did their best to learn their lines, but Johnathon worked the hardest of all. He walked around the room reciting lines; he said the lines at lunch; and he even practiced his part when he was supposed to be working, quietly, at his desk. I couldn't scold him, because he was so good! He had a cause, and he was determined to do his best, whatever the cost. I know I was prejudiced that year when Johnathon was preparing to be Peter Rabbit. But he was absolutely wonderful! Each time we practiced, the other students were held spell-bound with his performance. Many of the faculty and staff members heard about Johnathon's acting ability and used their planning times to come to the cafeteria to watch him practice. Johnathon became the talk of the school, and everyone could not wait for the night of the performance.

On the day before "Peter Rabbit" was to debut, Mr. Bill brought Johnathon to school. Instead of letting him out at the entrance of the school as he usually did, he parked and came into the building. When I headed down the hall to my classroom that morning, I panicked. There stood Johnathon with Mr. Bill in front of my doorway.

"Is anything wrong, Mr. Bill?" I looked from Johnathon to the kindly, old gentleman who worked for the home where Johnathon was staying.

"Well, I don't think so, Mrs. Harris. I just need to talk to you a bit before you go in if you don't mind. Johnathon, you go on in and sit down while I talk to your teacher a minute." Mr. Bill gently put his hand on Johnathon's shoulder and nudged him through the doorway. Johnathon looked at me briefly, dropped his head, and went in the room to his desk.

With a feeling of dread, I eased my bookbag to the floor and supported my trembling body with the wall. "What's wrong, Mr. Bill? Johnathon looks like he's seen a ghost!"

"Well, Mrs. Harris, I have some rather bad news. The trial for Johnathon's mother has been moved up. It is scheduled to go before the courts tomorrow."

"What! That can't be! I know for a fact that her trial was scheduled for the first week of June! What happened?"

"I don't rightly know, Ma'am. We just got a call this morning that they moved her date up to tomorrow morning. I know that's the day of your play and all, but Johnathon's going to have to be in court tomorrow to testify to what happened and all. I'm awfully sorry, Ma'am. We were planning to bring all the other children to see the play tomorrow night. If the case comes up early tomorrow, we'll still be able to make it to the play. I just know that the jury will find her guilty, and she will go straight back to jail for what she did to those boys. They might not even get to her case tomorrow. I've been to plenty of these proceedings at the courthouse, and they always drag out for several days. I don't think you have to worry, Mrs. Harris. I just wanted to tell you what was going on, since Johnathon has the lead part in the play and all, and to let you know that he won't be in school tomorrow since he will have to be in court."

"I guess Johnathon knows what's going on, " I ventured. "He didn't look too happy when he went in the room a while ago."

"No, Ma'am, he's really worried. But we had to tell him. I just hate that we had to spoil his excitement over the play, but we didn't have a choice. He is the only one who can tell what really happened the night he and his little brother were hurt so badly. He has to be in court. I'd give anything if it was another day. But as soon as they are finished with him, I promise you that I will bring him right over to the school. He's going to be 'Peter Rabbit' if it's the last thing that I do!"

EIGHTEEN

JOHNATHON DID SHOW UP at school the next day. Right after lunch, when the other children were getting into their outfits for the dress rehearsal, there was a knock at the door. Tara ran to open the door and yelled, " Miz Harris! Miz Harris! Johnathon's here! Johnathon's here to be Peter!"

But Johnathon never got to play the part of "Peter Rabbit" that day. When I went to the door, there he stood with his mother! She was propped on one foot, holding little Willie on her hip. I just stopped in my tracks and stared! I couldn't say a word!

"You must be Johnathon's teacher. Well, he needs to get his things, 'cause we're leaving this crummy town for good! Go on, Johnathon! Get your things so we can go!"

Johnathon never looked up as he slowly walked over to his desk and got his tablet and papers from inside his desk. The other children stopped what they were doing and watched in silence as the lead in the play and their friend walked out of the room and out of their lives for good. Johnathon eased past me to where his mother was standing. Tears streamed down my face as I put my hand out to touch Johnathon on the shoulder. He reached up and put his little hand over mine. He looked up at me, his big, brown eyes sad, almost beyond recognition.

"Bye, Techr. I love you." With that, Johnathon turned and walked down the hall and out the door of the school. In my heart I felt that I would never see him again.

The play went on as scheduled that night. Todd played the part of "Peter Rabbit," and everyone said it was a good play. I really don't know how it turned out. I was so filled with grief over the loss of Johnathon that I couldn't think about anything else.

I found out later that Johnathon's mother was found guilty of child abuse by the jury, but because of Johnathon's testimony in favor of his mother, the judge sentenced her to the time she had already served and gave the children back to her with a stiff warning to be 'a little more careful in her way of disciplining the boys.' In my opinion, the United States judicial system that was set up by our forefathers to protect the innocent, let three, trusting citizens down that day. Not only were my Johnathon and little Willie sentenced to a life of abuse and neglect, but I lost my enthusiasm to fight for the lost and unloved and downtrodden in this world. It was a long time before I ever let myself get that close to a child again. Well, at least until the next year when a whole new crop of students came into my life again!

NINETEEN

THE LAST TWO WEEKS of school that year passed as if time had almost come to a standstill. The students and I literally mourned the loss of Johnathon from the group, and everyday we hoped beyond hope that he would somehow find his way back into our little class. But he didn't.

The school year ended on a bleak note as I hugged all of my students for the last time on the final day of school. Tearfully, I told each of them good-bye and wished them all well for the next year. But I could not shake the feeling that I had missed giving a hug and farewell to the one little boy who needed it most of all. I prayed that some teacher, somewhere, hugged Johnathon that day, if, in fact, he was even in school.

The summer passed much too quickly, and it was not long before I started to see most of the children from that class in the second grade with their new teachers. They always spoke to me in the halls, but I never heard that dearest voice of all say, "Hey, Techr."

A few weeks after the new school year began, I found out that Johnathon had moved to a town near the coast when the school there requested his records. I wrote to him many times, but my letters were all returned with "Address Unknown" stamped on them. I guess his mother was constantly moving from place to place. I finally heard that Johnathon had been taken from his home again and put in another foster home somewhere in the lower part of the state. I tried, desperately, to find where he was, but each time I got a new clue as to his whereabouts, he would move again. I finally lost track of him altogether. For a long time, I wondered how he turned out, and every night I prayed to the Lord to keep little Johnathon in His care.

One year blended into another as I embraced new first-graders, year after year. I continued to teach my little charges to read, even though the techniques changed about as fast as I could learn them myself.

To tell the truth, I was plenty scared when the advent of computer technology hit the schools, but I somehow managed to move with the times and learned how to maneuver a "mouse," dial up on a modem, and "surf the net" with the best! I must admit, however, that I did pray an awful lot during those days!

After thirty-five years of teaching first grade in the same room of the same school, I started having heart problems. At first I thought it was indigestion, but when my usual Tums didn't do the trick, I went to the doctor. Dr. Bob, who had been the town doctor for as long as I could remember, told me that the old ticker was not getting the blood it needed to work properly due to three clogged arteries leading to the heart.

I looked down at my rather plump body and sighed. When had I let myself gain so much weight? I decided it was probably after Will died when I started eating lunch everyday in the school cafeteria. It was most likely all those french fries I had been eating for several years that did it.

Dr. Bob said that he could not perform the triple by-pass that I needed, and so he sent me to Atlanta, Georgia, to have the surgery. I figured my condition must be pretty bad when I was flown by helicopter, directly to the hospital.

It was a scary feeling being in a strange place awaiting serious heart surgery by a doctor I had never seen in my life. I wished many times that Will was still alive to be with me, but he had been dead for three years. I was all alone in the world except for the students in my first grade back home.

I had not been at the hospital long when all sorts of nurses and other medical people came and took blood and ran every kind of test imaginable on me. They all appeared to be in a hurry, and no one seemed to have time to answer my questions or calm my fears. I kept asking about the doctor who would perform my surgery, and I was told, curtly, that a Dr. Adams, who would be my surgeon, had been called in and should be arriving shortly.

In no time flat, I was wheeled into a room adjacent to the operating room to await my surgery. I had not been given anything, at that point, to put me to sleep, so I was fully alert when a tall, good-looking doctor in his mid-thirties walked into the room. He had on his operating attire; a green suit of some sort, a green cover for his head, and cover-ups over his shoes. He had a stethoscope around his neck and surgical glasses over his eyes. He walked over to my bed and reached down and took my hand.

"Good morning. I'm Dr. Adams, but most people call me Dr. John. I will be performing the triple by-pass surgery on you today. Are you all ready to get this behind you?"

I looked at this young man who was half my age and felt a tremor of fear go up and down my spine. "To tell you the truth, Doctor, I'm really scared. I'm not young, you know, and I've never been sick in my life, to speak of, so I'm really scared. Can you promise me that I will be all right when the operation is over? Everybody's been rushing around me so much. I really am scared to death!"

"Oh, don't you worry one little bit! I'm going to fix you up as good as new. You'll feel like a young person again when I finish with you. So, don't you worry."

I looked at the kind, brown eyes of the young doctor, and for a brief moment I felt like I had seen those eyes before. I knew it wasn't possible, but I also felt like I had heard that voice before, too. I didn't realize I was staring at the doctor until I heard him laugh.

"You're looking at me funny. I don't believe you remember me, do you,........Techr?"

I tried to focus on the handsome face before me...the mouth...the crooked smile...and the eyes...big, bright, brown eyes! I clasped my hands together as I looked into those familiar eyes! My mouth dropped open. It couldn't be!

"Do you remember a little, ragtag boy who walked into your first grade class about thirty years ago? Well, I'm that little boy, Techr. I'm Johnathon!"

I stared at the familiar face, and in a flash of a second, I was back, standing in my classroom, with a little, dirty, pathetic boy tapping on my leg and saying, "Are you my techr? I'm Johnathon." I blinked my eyes and came back to the present. Johnathon! My Johnathon! This handsome, important, CLEAN, doctor was my Johnathon!

Johnathon looked down at me and smiled. "You know something, Techr? When nobody listened to me, you did. When nobody had time for me, you had time for me. When no one cared about me, Techr, you cared. And when no one loved me, Techr, you loved me."

Tears rolled down my cheeks as I listened to Johnathon. He gently reached over and wiped the tears away with his strong, important, doctor's hand. All I could think about was the little, grimy hand that used to touch my face so often.

"Techr, you started to build me a future that first day I walked into your class. And, oh, what a future it's been, Techr. Look at me! I'm a surgeon, a heart surgeon! It's all because of you, Techr. You gave me a chance, and you believed in me. You gave me a future, Techr, and so today, I'm going to give some of your future back to you. And you don't have to worry, Techr. I would never let anything happen to you. I have to get you well, because I believe that you still have a lot of love in that heart of yours to give to some other little boy or girl."

I stared at my Johnathon in disbelief! I had finally found him after all these years. I couldn't believe it! My Johnathon was a doctor! My doctor! Suddenly, I was not scared at all. All I could do was hold on to Johnathon's strong hand; the same hand that would soon be fixing up that old heart of mine, and I smiled.

Johnathon leaned over my bed and looked right in my eyes. "You know something, Techr. When you are all better, I want you to walk down the corridor of the hospital to the end of the hall. I have an office there, and there's something sitting on my desk that I want you to see. Can you guess what it is?"

I shook my head as I listened to this dear boy. I couldn't imagine what he had to show me.

"Well, Techr, there is a little doctor's kit sitting on my desk, and it has been there since the day I became a doctor. Do you remember it, Techr? You should. You gave it to me that Christmas when I didn't get anything. You know something, Techr? It took me a long time to figure out that you gave me that little kit and not Santa Claus!"

I smiled through my tears as I thought back to that Christmas so long ago. I did remember the little doctor's kit. I only paid $2.99 for it, but Johnathon had acted like it was made of gold.

"Ah, Techr! You sure did make a difference in my life! I don't know what would have happened to me, Techr, if you had not cared about me. Thank you, Techr! Thank you for building me a future! I love you Techr!"

A few minutes later, I was wheeled into the operating room with my dear Johnathon walking right beside me, holding my hand. The last image in my mind as the anesthesia dulled my senses was of a little, ragtag boy, looking up at me with big, brown eyes and calling me, "Techr."

TWENTY

JOHNATHON WAS TRUE to his word. He did fix my old heart, and it wasn't any time before I was up and about, ready to face the rest of my future. Every afternoon, Johnathon came and walked with me up and down the halls of the hospital. I noticed several of the nurses and other doctors watching us as we strolled, arm in arm, and they probably wondered about the attraction of the young doctor to the old teacher. I could have told them the story about Johnathon, but I doubt that they would have believed it.

Before I left the hospital, I went down to Johnathon's office and saw the little doctor's kit sitting on his big desk. He had it proudly displayed on a gleaming, gold pedestal like it was the most important possession he owned. Perhaps it was.

Two weeks after my surgery, I had to say good-bye to Johnathon once again. He refused to let the nurses' aide take me to the ground floor where a friend of mine was waiting to drive me back to South Carolina. He helped me in the wheel chair and pushed me himself. I felt like a queen as everyone on the floor stopped to watch the important surgeon wheel me to the elevator.

When we reached my friend's car, Johnathon put my little suitcase in the trunk and turned to face me. "Techr, you take care now, and follow all of my instructions. Don't do anything too strenuous, and watch your diet. No more french fries, you hear?"

I made a mock salute to Johnathon as I listened to all the orders he repeated for the umpteenth time. "Don't worry about me, Johnathon. I'll be fine. You take care, too, and don't work too hard."

Tears filled my eyes as Johnathon reached down and hugged me. "I'll keep in touch, Techr. If I ever get any time off, I'll try to come and see you. I love you, Techr."

"I love you, too, Johnathon." I bravely smiled, got in the car, and drove away. I figured that would be the last time I would ever see Johnathon.

After several weeks of resting at home and following Johnathon's strict orders, I went back to school to my little class of first graders. It was already May, so I only had a few weeks to go before the summer break.

I wrote to Johnathon several times that summer. I thanked him over and over for the operation that had literally saved my life. I did receive two postcards from him , and he even called me on my birthday. I guess he must have gotten the date from my hospital records.

Finally, the long, lonely summer passed, and a new school year beckoned me back to school. I got busy with my new students and tried to put Johnathon out of my mind. After all, he was an important, busy surgeon who didn't have time to keep up with his old, first grade teacher.

The busy weeks flew by, and before I knew it, the Christmas holidays were upon me. After sending my excited children off for their magical, two week break, I packed up my things and headed to my home across town. The holidays held no magic for me. I really dreaded spending two weeks, especially at that time of the year, all alone.

The days were endless as Christmas slowly approached. At first, I thought I wouldn't even put up a tree. After all, I would be the only one to see it since I didn't have a husband or a child to enjoy it with me. But the day before Christmas, I felt a strong urge to go and get a little tree.

Most of the good trees were gone by the time I got to the tree farm, but I finally spotted a little green fir that would fit in my car. I took it home, and put it in the old tree stand that Will and I had used for thirty-two years. I dug out the decorations and put them in the floor of the den. Memories flooded my brain as I held each precious ornament in my hands.

I lovingly hung the glossy, white bell that Will had given to me the first year we were married. I smiled at the gaudy, blue ornaments that my mother had insisted on passing down to me to use for our tree. Several of the colored balls were from my teacher friends at school, and there were at least a dozen, satin ornaments with the different years glued on in glitter. I chuckled when I remembered how many times I had helped Mrs. Rice frantically prepare the glittered balls for the faculty members at the last minute.

I had about finished decorating the tree, when something in the bottom of the ornament box caught my eye. I reached in and took out an old, tattered, papier-mache' dog. It had a little, round body and legs made out of popcicle sticks. It was partially colored with a black crayon and had a red collar with the letters, "GRG," on it.

I didn't have to think very hard to remember when this little, misshapen, roughly-made dog had joined my collection of Christmas ornaments. Johnathon had made this child's replica of his dog, George, right before that horrible Christmas when George was hit by a car. I held the tattered ornament to my heart and silently wept tears of sadness for the little boy who had survived a childhood with no Santa Claus, no Christmas trees, and no love, except for that of an old hound dog and a first grade teacher.

Then I remembered the man, Johnathon, and I cried tears of joy for the miraculous way Johnathon had beat the odds and acquired success in spite of everything. The last thing I recall that Christmas Eve night was holding on to Johnathon's little papier-mache' dog and remembering the little boy who had been the closest thing to a son that I would ever have.

I thought I was dreaming when I heard someone knocking on my door. I roused from a deep sleep and discovered I was still on the floor in a cramped position near the Christmas tree. The knock at the door got louder. I looked at the clock on the mantle. It was nine o'clock on

Christmas morning. I couldn't imagine who would be coming by to see me so early on Christmas Day.

I smoothed down my wrinkled clothes and called through the door. "Who's there?" When no one answered, I asked again. "Who's there?" When no answer came again, I peaked through the curtain to see who was at the door.

I couldn't believe my eyes! There stood Johnathon, loaded down with packages all decorated in brightly colored paper. I jerked open the door and clasped my hands over my mouth.

"Merry Christmas, Techr! I hope you don't mind me showing up like this, but I just had to come! You know, Christmas is a time for families, and you're the closest thing I have to a mother, so I just had to come and spend Christmas with you! Besides, I think it's time for my wife and two children to meet you, Techr!"

"Your wife....and....children? Johnathon, you didn't tell me you had a family!"

"I wanted to surprise you, Techr! My wife, Leigh, and I have been planning to come here for Christmas if I could take the time off, and we wanted to surprise you! So, here we are!" Johnathon dropped his packages on the floor of the porch and grabbed me in a great, big, bear hug.

When I could finally catch my breath, I looked past Johnathon to the long, white van parked at my front steps. "Well, Johnathon, tell your family to get out of the car and come on in!"

Johnathon turned and motioned with his hand for the people in the car to come to the porch. I watched in awe as the door of the van opened, and a tall, slim, beautiful girl stepped out. She waved at me like I was a long, lost friend. My heart was about to burst as I looked from Johnathon to this lovely girl who had to be Leigh.

Johnathon smiled at me and winked. "That's Leigh, my wife, Techr. I did pretty well for myself, didn't I?"

I nodded my head as I watched the back door of the van slide open. A little girl with brown, curly hair stepped out first. She walked up to where I was standing and stood, shyly, beside her father.

"Techr, this is Tara, our oldest child. She is eight and in the third grade."

I looked at Johnathon as I suddenly remembered another little girl with long, brown hair named Tara.

Johnathon saw the look on my face and smiled. "Yes, Techr. I named her. I always did like the name, Tara."

"Well, how do you do, Tara? I'm Mrs. Harris. I'm so very glad to meet you." Tara looked at me and smiled, but didn't answer. I recognized from years of experience with children, that she needed some time to get to know me, so I didn't push her. Johnathon reached down and took his daughter's hand.

"We got the children up real early this morning and drove several hours to get here to spend Christmas with you, Techr. Tara's real tired, but she'll warm up to you before long."

As I smiled and nodded to Johnathon, I felt someone tap me on the leg. I looked down into the same little face that had haunted me for so many years! A little boy with bright, brown eyes, much too large for his little, round face, stood with pigeon-toed feet, lightly tapping my leg. He was wearing a brand new Braves tee shirt and a shiny, blue cap. He had on crisp, new jeans, that fit him perfectly, and fancy, white sneakers on his feet. I closed my eyes and looked up to the heavens, thanking God for my good fortune, when I felt another tap on my leg. A crooked smile came on the little boy's face as I looked back down at him.

"Are you Techr?" the child asked, shyly, easing his little finger into his mouth. "I'm Johnathon."